Star-Crossed Miracles

Masters of the Prairie Winds Club
Book Nine

by Avery Gale

Copyright © 2018 by Avery Gale
ISBN 978-1-944472-47-4
All cover art and logo © Copyright 2018 by Avery Gale
All rights reserved.

The Masters of the Prairie Winds Club® and Avery Gale® are registered trademarks

Cover Design by Jess Buffett
Published by Avery Gale

Thank you for respecting the hard work of this author.

This is a work of fiction. Names, places, characters and incidents either are the product of the author's imagination or are used fictitiously and any resemblance to any actual persons, living or dead, organizations, events or locales are entirely coincidental.

No part of this book may be reproduced, stored in a retrieval system, or transmitted by any means without the written permission of the author and publishing company.

WARNING: The unauthorized reproduction or distribution of this copyrighted work is illegal. Criminal copyright infringement, including infringement without monetary gain, is investigated by the FBI and is punishable by up to 5 years in federal prison and a fine of $250,000.

If you find any books being sold or shared illegally, please contact the author at avery.gale@ymail.com.

Prologue

Mia Lucrezia Borgia Mendez crouched under the thick ferns high in the Colombian mountains and zoomed her camera in on the emaciated man chained in the center of the compound she'd finally found. She'd spent the last several months chasing rumors of an American político being held captive, and now that she'd finally found him, she had to remind herself to stay focused and do her job. Taking a deep breath, she concentrated on getting the clear shots she'd need if she wanted to make a case to the media outlets she usually sold to.

Haunted eyes—sunken in so far, she wondered if his captors were intentionally torturing him with starvation—looked out from under straggly, matted hair. The entire encampment was eerily silent, and Mia knew she only had a few more seconds before she was discovered. Slipping the secondary memory chip from her camera, Mia secured it in the small pocket she'd stitched in the lining of her jacket. Anyone attempting to steal the shots would assume the chip they found in her camera would hold all the evidence. A flurry of activity on the other side of the camp led to an eruption of gunfire in the distance. In the split second before she slipped back into the heavy cover of the forest, Mia watched a young woman sprint from a nearby hut. She shoved a heavy key into the lock securing the man and pulled him to his feet.

Mia stood frozen in place watching as the woman appeared to be speaking rapidly to the man who staggered until he eventually appeared to gain his footing. The chain securing him to the post had been too short for him to stand, so Mia knew his legs had to have been weakened. Before her common sense could overrule her heart, Mia rushed forward to help the young woman carry the man into the heavy forest cover.

The three of them stumbled to where Mia had hidden the small truck she'd borrowed from her landlord. Quickly covering the two fugitives with the heavy tarps in the truck bed, Mia drove as fast as the rutted road leading to the nearby village allowed. She'd only gone a mile or two before they'd come upon the larger truck the young woman had told her to watch for parked along the side of the heavily rutted road.

As Mia helped uncover her passengers from their hiding place, the man wrapped his large hand around her wrist and locked his gaze with hers. In his weakened state, he'd only been able to utter three words... *Senator... Doctor... U.S.*, but they'd been enough.

It hadn't taken Mia long to learn his identity when she'd been able to access the internet. Packing up her few belongings, Mia had paid her landlord a handsome bonus for the use of his truck and hopefully, his silence. She'd driven her own small car through the night to reach Cali before finally stopping to rest.

Slipping into the hotel's deserted business center before dawn, Mia printed the pictures and mailed them to the address she'd found online. Guilt weighed heavily on her as she tried to imagine the pain and uncertainty this disruption would cause the young doctor whose picture she'd seen online. The woman considered herself a widow, but

Mia believed Dr. Tally Tyson deserved the truth.

Mia's family had never understood her passion for photojournalism, but they usually indulged her, hoping she'd one day come to her senses and join the family business. But she'd always seen her work as a form of public service. She was a truth-seeker, but she understood the danger she'd just put herself in, and for the first time, Mia considered returning home for her own safety. The money she'd given her toothless landlord wouldn't hold his tongue for long. She wasn't naïve enough to believe the criminal faction who'd been holding the American politician wasn't already hot on her heels and would eventually track her down if she wasn't careful.

She wondered who the woman was who'd helped him escape. For all Mia knew, she'd simply helped him jump from the frying pan into the fire. There wasn't any question Mia's family could and would protect her, but it would come at a cost… one far greater than she was willing to pay. And not everyone in her grandfather's employ would be thrilled to see her return.

Chapter One

Two Months later

MIA MENDEZ HUDDLED in the shallow space beneath the floorboards in her bedroom as the heavy steps of booted feet passed inches above her. The way they stomped told her they hadn't expected her to be in the small one bedroom apartment she'd been renting for the past two months. Dios, they weren't even making a token attempt at stealth. It would be a miracle if her downstairs neighbor didn't call the local police… not that it would do any good. Mia had lived in Columbia her entire life and had yet to meet a public official who hadn't been either compromised, threatened, or killed by one of the cartels.

The man standing directly above her was obviously in charge. His barked orders spoken with an edge of urgency told her he wasn't looking forward to reporting back to his superiors if they failed to find what they were looking for. His promise of a night with one of 'the girls' for the man who found her laptop made her want to throw up. She wondered what she'd done to tip them off? Damn it to donuts, she'd managed to fly under their radar for so long, she'd evidently gotten careless.

Holding her breath as she watched the man through the ill-fitting boards, Mia cursed herself for not rearranging the bedroom. It had taken her most of the first week to fashion a hiding spot large enough to stash her 'go bag' and several more days to enlarge it enough for her to slip into. The finger holds were almost undetectable from above, and she'd barely had time to scramble inside when she'd heard numerous car doors slam outside on the street. She might have grown slack, but her survival instincts had kicked into high gear at the out-of-place sounds. The deserted street she lived on rarely had traffic of any kind, and several vehicles at one time had been a sure sign of trouble.

The sound of breaking glass made her suck in a quick, surprised breath, causing the man closest to her to call for silence. They all stopped moving for long seconds, and Mia held her breath so long, her vision started to dim. After what seemed like an eternity, the rag-tag group finally agreed to return later that night after she'd returned. It didn't take a genius to figure out how that would work out for her.

Mia remained hidden even after she heard vehicles speeding down the hard-packed dirt street, trying to slow her breathing and sort through her chaotic thoughts while planning her escape.

BROCK DEITZ EASED back, melting deeper into the shadows when the men who'd been searching Mia Mendez's small apartment began filing out of the building. He and his brother had been watching the apartment for the past four days. His brother, Tucker was spotting from the roof of the building at his back. Brock knew Tuck had kept the men in his rifle sights from the moment they'd arrived in force.

"She's quick, I'll give her that. Damn, she grabbed her

backpack and computer and was hidden before they made it up the first flight of stairs."

"The hidey-hole under the floor?" They'd found her safe space, but it hadn't been easy. Brock had to give Ms. Mendez credit, she was well prepared. Her go bag had a generous stash of cash and multiple sets of identification. He wondered if she'd created the space when she'd first arrived or if a recent incident had caused her to worry... like mailing pictures of Senator Tyson to his wife.

"Yeah. I thought for a few seconds they'd made her after one of the asshats broke a lamp, but they finally gave up and moved out." Tucker's voice held a hint of respect for the woman they both were starting to feel as if they knew despite the fact they had yet to meet her face to face.

Tuck, as he was known to family and close friends, had maintained a healthy distance from any woman who'd expressed even the smallest interest in him since his split from the witch he'd been married to for six harrowing months. If Brock never saw Jina Ives' cheating face again, it would be a lifetime too soon.

"I know we're only supposed to watch her until the rest of the team arrives late tonight, but I think that option was just taken off the table." Brock knew he was stating the obvious, but Tucker had been trying to downplay his interest in the woman they were shadowing, so Brock wanted to make sure his brother was on board upping their timetable.

"We're going to have to grab her—there won't be a safe place for her in the entire damned city."

Brock could tell by the sound of Tucker's voice he was already on the move. Within seconds Brock felt the faintest brush of air as Tucker stepped up beside him. Brock didn't respond to his presence, just nodded in the direction of the apartment building. They needed to get to Ms. Mendez before she decided to make a run for it—and he didn't have a doubt one that was exactly what she planned to do.

"Fuckers destroyed everything. They might have been looking for something, but this was also intended to send her a strong message," Tucker's comment surprised Brock. Ever since his divorce last year, Tucker had made every attempt to turn off any emotion vaguely resembling compassion.

"Well, message received. My guess is the simpletons expect her to be picking through the carnage when they return later tonight. She'd be distracted and easy to grab." Pushing out an exasperated breath, Brock moved from the shadows, the two of them crossed the street, and made their way up the stairs.

"Let's find her and get out of here. The more miles we can cover before they return, the better. Let the team and Prairie Winds know about the change in plans." Tucker pulled out his phone and began tapping a quick message.

Slipping into her apartment less than a minute later, Brock shook his head at the devastation. The first time they'd stepped into the young woman's home, it had been neat to the point of being impersonal. Now, however, the space looked like a tornado had gone through it—or their younger sister, Nell. Nellora was a one-woman wrecking crew. Brock had seen their mother scramble to stash treasured pieces of her crystal before Nell made her way into a room.

Brock moved to the bedroom and smiled when he saw the cover of her hiding place still securely in place. *It's time for us to finally meet, sweetheart.* Pulling the knife from the sheath around his ankle, he pushed the tip of the titanium blade between the slats of the rough-hewed floor and lifted the cover. He heard Mia's startled cry at the same moment his gaze met hers.

He'd expected her to be alarmed at having been discovered, what he hadn't anticipated was the startling crystal blue of her eyes. Her hair was so dark, even the dim light reflected from the shining strands that had pulled free of the long braid she wore. During the past couple of days, Brock had been forced to pull himself out of more than one fantasy where he threaded his fingers through the loose length of her silky hair. Damn, he wanted to see it loose and flowing around her slender shoulders.

"Come on, Mia." Extending his hand, he smiled down at her and nearly laughed out loud at her look of defiance. "We need to get you out of here." When she didn't immediately take his offered hand, he frowned. "My brother and I have been sent to help you, but we're going to need your cooperation. You and I both know the men who just left here will be coming back, and you can't hide in here forever."

A flicker of acknowledgment shone in her eyes, and she started to grasp his hand, but just before he could grasp it, she pulled it back.

"How did you know where I was? You walked right to this spot."

"We found your little safe space the first time we checked your room when we got to town. It's well hidden, but it's not impossible to find. Even the morons who trashed your apartment will find it, eventually." For the first time since he'd pried the boards away to uncover her, Brock saw a very real flash of terror in her eyes. She started to reach for his hand once again but pulled it back when she heard footsteps in the hall.

Tuck stepped into the room and frowned when he saw

Mia was still tucked into her hiding spot.

"What's the fucking hold up? We need to roll." Closing the distance between them, Tucker moved into Mia's view, and Brock heard her quick inhalation when she saw Tuck for the first time. He and his brother were only ten months apart in age and looked enough alike to be twins—*almost*.

Tucker's bright green eyes were always the first thing people noticed. Strangers on the street would stop and stare at him when Tucker had been a child, much to the dismay of their parents. His eyes were so memorable, Tuck was forced to wear colored contacts on missions to avoid drawing undue attention to himself.

"You said you were sent to help me… who sent you and why?"

Brock smiled at her question. *Thought you'd never ask, baby.* He'd wondered if she was going to overlook the most obvious questions and was relieved to know she was cognizant enough to be thinking about her own safety.

"Come on, Mia, let's get you somewhere safe, then we'll talk about who sent us. For now, all you need to know is we're the good guys."

This time she took his proffered hand despite Tuck's snort of derision at his words. Brock was amused at the way she shimmied out of the small space. When she turned and started to reach back into the hole, Brock wrapped his arm around her waist and pulled her back until she was flush against his torso. The lush curves of her ass pressed against his groin, and he barely stifled his groan at the surge of blood rushing to fill his rapidly inflating cock.

Leaning down, Brock spoke softly against the sensitive skin behind her ear, "Let Tuck retrieve your things, sweetheart, while you and I take a quick look around. Let's see if there is anything left you'd like to take, shall we?"

He'd inhaled deeply and almost moaned as the sweet smell of her skin filled his senses. A surge of electricity raced up his spine when his lips brushed over her tanned skin, and satisfaction warmed him when she shivered in his embrace. She didn't immediately move away when he released her, and he fought the urge to turn her, so he'd be able to feel the soft press of her pillowy breasts against his chest.

When she finally stepped away from him, Brock had to turn away to readjust himself. If that brief moment of contact had such a profound effect, what would it be like to have Mia sandwiched between him and Tuck? Turning back to her, Brock smiled when he saw her on her hands and knees, her luscious ass pointing in the air as she pulled a second bag from its hiding place under her bed. He was enjoying the hell out of the view when Tuck moved to his side.

"Jesus," the single, almost reverent epitaph summed up Brock's sentiments perfectly.

Chapter Two

THEY'D BEEN ON the road for an hour, and Tucker Deitz still hadn't been able to scrub the image of Mia's perfectly rounded ass from his mind. *Hell, that fucking mental picture is burned into my brain for all eternity.* More than once, he'd nearly driven off the damned road just picturing it in his mind. He was certain she hadn't given a second thought to the view she'd given them when she'd been on all fours, and for the first time in a year, his cock had completely forgotten about his scheming ex-wife.

As devastating as Jina's betrayal had been, enduring his brother's reminders about all the ways he'd tried to warn him had been almost as painful. And the very worst part—Brock had been right all along. In the beginning, Tucker had been convinced his brother was just jealous because Jina had chosen him over the polyamorous relationship they'd always planned if they found the right woman. He'd been wrong, Jina had known she couldn't fool Brock, but Tuck had fallen for her lies—hook, line, and sinker.

Tucker and Brock had planned to share a wife, but Brock had disliked Jina from the moment the two met and hadn't made any attempt to hide his contempt for her. She'd eventually convinced Tucker that Brock's envy was the issue, and since he'd been thinking with his dick instead of his head, he'd believed her.

Within weeks of their marriage, Tucker knew he'd

made a mistake. He moved out of their bedroom the first time he caught her cheating, but his pride kept him in the marriage for four more torturous months. By the time he officially ended the sham, he'd become so cold and bitter, most women sensed his disdain and avoided him like the plague. Hell, even subs at the club who cared about nothing more than the mind-blowing orgasms he could give them walked a wide circle around him if Brock wasn't part of the equation.

Glancing over his shoulder to where Mia lay sleeping peacefully, Tucker shook his head, trying to keep the lustful thoughts from creeping back in. His first look at Mia Mendez had been through a rifle scope, and she'd still managed to shake him to his core. He was still trying to figure out what the hell it was about her that had caused his reaction.

"You're thinking so fucking hard, it's giving *me* a headache." Brock's low-pitched voice brought Tucker back to the moment. "Is your attraction to her such a bad thing?"

Leave it to Brock to cut straight to the heart of something. Damn, he'd been like this their entire lives, and to make matters worse, his brother was one of the most intuitive people Tucker had ever met. Why he'd failed to listen to Brock's warnings about Jina was a fucking mystery Tucker was convinced he'd never unravel.

"Yes," sighing, Tucker finally answered his brother's question. "No. Fuck, I don't know. Maybe not, but I wasn't prepared for it."

"Just because you didn't see something coming doesn't always mean it's negative. Let's set aside your confusion for now and focus on protecting her." Brock shifted in his reclining position and turned in his seat to face Tucker. The intense scrutiny made Tucker uncomfortable, and he finally turned to glare at his brother. "All I'm asking is to table this discussion until Mia is safe."

Tucker knew better. His brother might think he'd done a good job of masking his interest, but his blasé attitude was so ridiculously transparent, Tucker almost laughed out loud. Keeping his voice lowered to avoid waking Mia, Tucker replied, "Agreed, but I'm warning you now, brother, don't mistake my attraction to her for something more. We're here to keep her safe and nothing more."

BROCK SIGHED ALOUD even as he was cursing under his breath. His brother wasn't going to easily acknowledge his obvious attraction. Hell, he'd seen the look on Tuck's face when he'd pulled Mia from her hiding place and known, instantly, the little bundle of blue-eyed innocence had reignited the inner flame of desire Tucker was convinced Jina had doused into extinction.

Deciding it was time to redirect the conversation, Brock pulled out their SAT phone and placed a call to Prairie Winds. After explaining what had transpired to Kent and Kyle West, Brock listened as his bosses shared the new information they'd received about the woman in the backseat. The tone of Kyle's voice was pitched low and the cadence slowed, both signaling the seriousness of what he was sharing.

"Your passenger is none other than Mia Lucrezia Borgia Mendez. She can trace her family history back to Pope Alexander VI."

"Did you say Pope?" Brock might not be Catholic, but even he knew Popes were supposed to be unmarried and celibate.

"There are periods of corruption in all the great religions, and this is one of those times that has been openly acknowledged and discussed for many years. As the product of a poly-marriage who shares a wife with my twin brother, I'm not in any position to judge, but from the sounds of it, this guy was quite a lover."

Brock chuckled because he'd forgotten Kent and Kyle's parents had shocked their family and friends when Dean and Dell West married Lilly.

"Anyway, one of Pope Alexander VI's children was Lucrezia Borgia, a Duchess several times over—whatever the hell that means. She is Mia's great-something or other grandmother and her namesake. The bottom line is her involvement is going to add a whole new level of public interest when this story breaks, and it will."

"Fast forward five hundred plus years, and we have Mia," Kent picked up where Kyle left off. "Her family's wealth is staggering. Her grandfather owns most of the banks in Columbia, but she appears to be resisting their efforts to wrap her in cotton and set her on a shelf."

A thousand questions raced through Brock's mind. Why hadn't she used her family's connections to contact Tally instead of simply mailing the photos? Did her family know she was in trouble? Would they try to keep her from helping them find Senator Tyson? Were the men in her apartment part of the cartel suspected of holding the senator or a retrieval team sent in by her family? One of their contingency plans had been to transport Mia back to Prairie Winds in the hope she would be able to help the team remotely. But now, Brock wasn't sure she'd even be interested in leaving.

"Listen, we just received a new piece of intel we haven't been able to confirm, but if it's true, you need to be aware. It seems there are likely at least three different factions looking for her. The first is the cartel, who knows she's a photojournalist and that she was the woman who helped the second group of banditos snatch Karl Tyson out from under their noses. Now, because the Cartel is waving some serious cash around in their search for Ms. Mendez and the good Senator, you have mercs inciting a bidding war for the recovery of Ms. Mendez and her photos. And just to keep things interesting, her grandfather also has a team looking for her, albeit they are evidently keeping a much lower profile for obvious reasons.

Letting out a low whistle and scrubbing his hand over his face before responding, Brock couldn't believe the mess they'd walked in to. "What a cluster-fuck." He didn't know what else to call it. They were at least two hours from the coast, and even if they made it to their destination, how were they going to secure her until they could find out what she knew.

"I'm sorry."

Brock whipped his head to the side and found Mia sitting up, staring at him, her sapphire blue eyes wide and filled with guilt. Brock couldn't remember a time he felt more like an ass than he did now.

"Find us a place to stay in Cartagena and transport out if you can." Brock was ready to disconnect when he heard a voice in the background.

"Wait. Micah says to tell you he's got something in the works, but your passenger is going to have to be open-minded. He's going to text you the info." Before Brock could ask what he meant, Kyle cut the connection, which caused Tucker to raise a brow in question. *I'm with you, brother. No fucking clue.* But the one thing Brock was certain of, if Micah Drake said Mia would need to keep an open mind, then there was kink involved. And if Drake was setting it up, the kink would be over the top—way over the fucking top, and *that* you could take to bank... pun intended.

Chapter Three

MIA SENT UP a silent prayer of thanks for all the practice she'd had pretending to sleep. Living under her grandfather's roof meant enduring an endless string of nannies and security personnel who only let their guard down when they thought she'd fallen asleep. Faking it turned out to be an invaluable skill when she'd gotten old enough to plot breakouts from what she not-so-affectionately referred to as kiddie-prison. If those charged with watching over her thought she was sleeping, they left her alone, and all the secondary escape routes her grandfather had in place for her 'safety' worked equally well for her convenience.

Listening to the two men in the front seat discuss their mutual attraction to her made Mia's body heat from the inside and sent a rush of moisture to slicken the throbbing folds of her sex. Barely resisting the urge to press her hand against her aching clit, Mia bit the inside of her cheek to stifle her moan of frustration. Her reaction was made even more unsettling by the fact these two men were obviously into menagé… something she'd only read about in the books on her e-reader. Her immediate response to them had annoyed her, but hearing she'd had the same effect on them lessened the sting. Well, at least she'd felt marginally better until she realized how much it had also unsettled the man named Tucker. *And why is that so humiliating?*

Listening as Brock spoke on the phone, she wanted to laugh at his effort to speak softly when whoever he was talking to was practically rattling the windows of the truck. It always surprised her when people failed to realize how clearly their conversations could be overheard... *both sides of their conversations.*

She'd often wondered what men were thinking, berating their wives and girlfriends over the phone when everyone near the woman could plainly hear what was being said. Most people kept the volume on their electronics loud enough to be heard in the next room, and they forgot that meant the voice of their caller was also amplified.

Mia wondered who Micah was and what exactly he meant when he'd said she needed to keep an open mind. Mia wasn't surprised they'd already connected her to Borgia Banking. Her grandfather was a self-made billionaire several times over and practically a legend in not only his own country but most of the Western Hemisphere as well. Mia loved her grandpapa more than she could possibly tell him. But after her grandmother's death, his love had felt conditional... every touch, every gift, every word of praise had come with strings.

Mia had never been interested in giving up everything she loved about her life to become the perfect princess she'd need to be for him to love her with the same soul-bearing depth she'd always shown him.

No matter how many times Mia's mother tried, she'd never been able to please her father, and Mia often wondered if she hadn't died of a broken heart from the constant rejection? Maria Mendez had left Mia in the care of her parents and traveled the world. When Mia had gotten older, she'd wondered if her mother had been searching for the love that always seemed just out of reach. The married man Maria had slept with resulting in Mia's birth had quickly retreated to the United States when he'd learned she was pregnant.

During Mia's last telephone conversation with her mother, Maria had whispered, "You can only try so hard, *amor*. Eventually, the desire for acceptance withers and dies, no matter how much you wish it wasn't so." Less than a week later, Maria died in Italy, and since Mia had never known her father, she was left adrift far too young.

The voices around her pulled Mia back to the present, and when the call Brock had made disconnected, she couldn't hold back her whispered apology. She saw Tucker's frown in the mirror and flinched. Brock turned in his seat and narrowed his eyes.

"What are you apologizing for, sweetheart? For finding a man all of us had given up for dead? For being brave enough to send the evidence to the one person guaranteed to call in a team to rescue him? Or perhaps you're sorry you didn't contact the U.S. government who would have no doubt swept the entire thing under the rug and dispatched agents to silence you. Hell, maybe you're sorry you've painted a target on yourself so big, it can probably be seen from the fucking International Space Station."

"Enough," Tucker's single hissed word made Brock's head swivel to him before he raised a brow in question. "Don't be a dick. She thinks this is the first clusterfuck we've ever been involved in, and you're being a first-class ass by pointing out points we both know she isn't sorry for."

Glancing at her over his shoulder, Tucker gave her a small smile, and even though it was a minimal effort, she was startled at how it completely transformed his appearance. Tucker returned his attention to the road, but Mia couldn't stop staring at his profile. If a man could be classified as fallen-angel beautiful, Tucker was the poster child.

"Asshole. One smile and she can't stop looking at you. I just don't fucking get it," Brock's words were harsh, but she could hear the underlying affection in them and let out a small sigh of relief. He turned around in his seat and helped her up into a sitting position.

"I'm sorry, Mia. I really wasn't trying to hurt your feelings. I was just looking forward to being able to kick back on the flight back to Texas and spend some time with you." He ran his hand through his hair and shook his head.

"Here's a tip, pointing out another person's flawed thinking isn't the best way to make friends and influence people." She'd barely finished speaking when Brock's head fell back and he roared with laughter. When she let her gaze slip to Tucker, she was surprised to see him chuckling as well.

"Damn, I think that's a first for me, sweetheart. I don't think I've ever been slapped with a Dale Carnegie book title before."

Dandy, she had to get rescued by a man who could actually read.

"We're going to have to stop for fuel before long. We'll eat at the same time, and that'll give you a chance to bring us up to speed on who all may be following you." She nodded at Brock, but he shook his head. "Not good enough, sweetheart. We'll always require you to speak your answers, that way there are no misunderstandings. We begin as we intend to go."

Reading was one of Mia's passions, and she'd read hundreds of erotic romance novels over the past few years, so Brock's words were hauntingly familiar. She felt a flash of heat that made her pussy wet and the muscles in her vagina tighten in response. Hopefully, the dim light in the vehicle would conceal the flush she could feel washing over her cheeks.

"Yes, Sir." The words tumbled out without passing through the filter in her brain. *Damn, so much for hiding that blush.*

BROCK WORRIED HIS oxygen-deprived brain was going to shut down at her whispered answer. Jesus, Joseph, and Mary, every drop of his blood rushed directly to his aching cock. The damned thing was going to burst at this rate. Tucker hadn't missed her sweet answer either, judging from the way his fingers flexed around the steering wheel. Both Deitz brothers had known they were sexual Dominants from the time they first became interested in the opposite sex. They didn't judge others for their sexual preferences, but other men had never set their blood racing like a naturally submissive woman did.

In the short time they'd spent hustling Mia out of her building before running two miles to where they'd hidden the truck, neither he nor Tucker had done much more than bark instructions at her. She'd done a good job of keeping up even though Brock knew she'd been exhausted. The one time he inquired if she needed to slow down, she muttered an apology, saying she hadn't been sleeping well, but she'd shaken her head when they offered to slow their pace. He wasn't surprised she wasn't resting, she must have known it was only a matter of time before she was found.

According to their intel, she didn't advertise her association with Cecilio Borgia, but she didn't try to hide it either. Brock figured she knew any attempt to conceal the connection would only draw more interest to it. The financial data Micah sent had been eye-opening. The woman sitting in the backseat, wearing what looked like well-worn, military tactical clothing was one of the world's wealthiest heiresses.

The frayed jacket made her look like a little girl playing dress up in her big brother's uniform. What on earth did she put in all those pockets, anyway? Maybe he should have frisked her for weapons before they left her cracker-box apartment. Just because she appeared to be a natural submissive, didn't mean they were safe. Shuddering, he remembered hearing Tobi West warn her husbands she'd shoot them with their own guns on more than one occasion.

"Good girl. Now, try to get a few more minutes of sleep. You're safe, and since we don't know what our team leaders are going to have set up for us when we hit the coast, you might not get another chance to rest for a while."

This time she didn't respond, simply settled back on to the seat and shifted her backpack over to use as a pillow. Not ideal, but probably better than the filthy leather seat, not to mention the fact the roads in Columbia were no match for those in the states—rough didn't even begin to cover it.

Following his own advice, Brock leaned his head back against the seat and closed his eyes. They always planned for contingencies when they went on any mission, but this one had been so time sensitive, they hadn't been able to pull as much intel together as was their usual protocol. Finding out they were dealing with threats from multiple sides came as something of a surprise. Personally, he'd rank the grandfather's team above the cartel, but not all families are as close as his, and hell, face it, there had to be a reason she hadn't gone back to the safety her grandfather could have provided.

Brock heard the phone beep beside him, but before he could push the cobwebs from his sleep-fogged mind, he heard Tucker speaking quietly into the small mic on his headset. Ordinarily, they'd bluetooth to the truck's speakers so they could both hear, but since they didn't know Mia well enough yet to fully trust her, they needed to play this with their cards a little closer to their chests.

Tucker sucked in a breath, and Brock straightened in his seat when he sensed his brother's agitation. "Jesus, is that all you've got?" Tuck listened for several long seconds and Brock wished like hell he knew what was being said. "Shit. There's so much wrong with this plan, I don't even know where to start. We're just pulling into Cartagena now, and I think we have enough fuel to make it to our destination, but we're all starving." After another few minutes of silence Tuck's "Roger that" indicated the end of the call.

Before Brock could ask, the phone dinged with an incoming message, and he saw Tucker pull up GPS coordinates. Handing the phone to Brock, Tucker sighed.

"You aren't going to fucking believe this. Grayson wasn't kidding when he said Mia is going to have to keep an open mind. Plug these in the system, will you?"

Brock quickly entered the data and raised a brow when he saw they were headed to the very western end of the docks. "Where are we going to eat?" Brock asked, giving his brother a questioning look. "We promised to feed her."

"On the ship. They're expecting us, and Kent has a

cleanup crew coming for the vehicle." Brock must have looked skeptical because Tucker shook his head. "We're going home in style, I'll say that." Brock sensed a very large *but* looming, so he didn't respond—he would just wait it out.

Tucker ran his hand through his hair in annoyance. The gesture was one of his younger brother's few 'tells,' and it always meant he was dancing on the edge of his limited patience. "The entire ship has been chartered by Cameron Barnes." This time it was Brock's turn to suck in a sharp breath.

"Are you fucking kidding me? The same Cameron Barnes who owns Dark Desire?" The owner of Houston's infamous kink club had become something of a recluse since moving to the Caribbean and helping his wife set up a much needed medical facility. From what Brock remembered, Dr. Cecelia Barnes was already famous in her own right when she married the club owner. Her innovations in pediatric surgery drew patients from all over the world to the clinic she'd established in Houston.

Tucker's voice broke through Brock's mental rehash of what he knew about Cameron Barnes. "Barnes chartered the entire ship as an anniversary gift for CeCe. Evidently, they are planning to add to their family again soon, and he wanted her to have a chance to fully indulge in her submission before she's pregnant."

"She does enjoy impact play," Brock chuckled, "and I know Cam is insanely protective even when she isn't pregnant. I don't even want to think about what he's like when she's carrying his child."

Brock and Tucker had both been members of the club for years, and they'd worked with Cam on a number of black op missions while they were SEALs despite the fact the man was supposed to be retired. Brock suspected Uncle Sam would never let Cam fully retire, he was simply too good at his job and knew too much to let him go.

Brock and Tuck had been heavily recruited by the CIA but turned down multiple offers because they'd heard too many stories like Cam's. As near as Brock could tell, the damned organization was too much like a blood-in, blood-out gang. Once you were a part of the group, death was your only way out.

Chapter Four

Tucker and Brock kept Mia between them as they walked through the large metal gate toward the dock. She'd evidently overheard enough of their conversation in the SUV to know they were getting on a ship; she hadn't questioned them when they turned into the large parking lot of the industrial end of the dock rather than continuing into the city as they'd originally planned. Tucker was beginning to worry about her continued silence, hell most of the women he knew would have been peppering them with questions.

As they approached a small building about halfway down the wooden dock's length, the shadowy figure of a man emerged from the small structure but remained in the shadows, leaning against the wall. *Cam Barnes.* Once a man was trained to remain in the shadows, it was an impossible habit to break. His stealth was legendary, and even those who knew him the best always wondered if they knew him at all.

When the trio reached the small office, Cam stepped out and offered his hand to Tucker and Brock. "Good to see you and under such interesting circumstances, too." Cam shook his head and smiled. "As usual, Micah's connections and timing are impeccable. If he'd called a few minutes later, we'd have already cast off, and it would have been damned hard to explain why we wanted to redock."

Turning his attention to Mia, Cam held out his hand, and even though she hesitated, she set her much smaller hand in his. "Mia, it's a pleasure to meet you. The men from Prairie Winds have told me a lot about you. My lovely wife is looking forward to meeting you, it seems your reputation as a photojournalist precedes you."

Mia's smile was warm, and even in the dim light, Tucker could see the pink blush of embarrassment staining her cheeks. *Fucking Barnes always could charm the ladies.*

"Come." Cam pressed a kiss to the back of her hand before gently tucking her small hand in the crook of his elbow. "There is no need to remain exposed any longer than necessary. My team has cleared the area, but drones have made it almost impossible to be certain we aren't being watched." As they walked, Cam gave them a quick run-down of the situation.

"The ship has six levels. We're using the top three for most of our activities and utilizing the next two floors exclusively for sleeping quarters because all those cabins are nicely appointed, spacious suites. We've assigned you one on the starboard side near the stern as an added precaution." His gaze flickered between Brock and Tucker, taking in the position of their hands and nodded. "Good. You're both right-handed. I took a chance you would be."

Tucker felt his lips curve at the adorably confused look on Mia's face. Since she clearly didn't have any military experience, she probably didn't understand how advantageous the position on the right side of the ship would be for a soldier holding a weapon in his or her right hand. His attention to detail was just one of the reasons Cam Barnes had attained an almost legendary status among covert operators the world over. Even his sworn enemies respected his intuitive ability to anticipate and intercept an adversary's next move.

In all the years Tucker had known Cam, he'd never seen him remotely ruffled professionally, but if anyone dared to endanger the woman standing in the distance, Cameron Barnes came apart at the seams. Carl Phillips loomed behind Dr. Cecelia Barnes, one arm wrapped securely around her upper torso, providing a perfect shelf that lifted her breasts perfectly, making it appear the mounds were dangerously close to spilling out of her low cut dress. As they approached, Carl leaned down and whispered something in CeCe's ear, and Tuck grinned when her entire body shuddered.

"Leave it to Carl to thoroughly distract her right before I need her focused," Cam chuckled. This time Mia's curiosity seemed to get the best of her and she opened her mouth to ask, but Cam gave her a small shake of his head. "I'll let my pet explain everything to you in a bit. We've already started spreading your cover story, and they'll be taking you up to the spa first. Right now, I need you to pay very close attention to your surroundings because your safety is our primary concern."

Tucker smiled when Cam paused until Mia's gaze returned to him, leaving Carl and CeCe to stand, waiting patiently at the end of the gangway. Mia surprised him when she finally turned her attention to Cam and tilted her head to the side.

"I have one question first, does everyone in your acquaintance share?"

Tucker could count on one hand the number of times he'd seen Cam Barnes do more than chuckle, so when Cam leaned his head back and laughed heartily, Tuck stared open-mouthed at him and wondered if hell had just frozen over.

Way to go, Mia. Open mouth and insert foot. The question had blindsided her, probably almost as it had their host. It was one of those moments when she opened her mouth, intending to say one thing and something else popped out. *I really do need to learn how to keep my thoughts and my words from playing scramble tag in my mind.* She'd meant to ask him if she'd be able to access the internet, so she could work while they were on board, but seeing the interaction between the man and woman standing in front of them had sent her mind reeling. *Dammit all to donut covered dalmatians, she hated it when that happened.*

"Mia, you and my wife are going to be fast friends, which is wonderful because that's how we're explaining your sudden appearance. We've already begun circulating the rumor that you have only been in the lifestyle for a short while and have recently become involved with the two Doms accompanying you. You sought your friend's advice on dealing with two men at the same time, and when CeCe learned you were close by on an assignment, she invited the three of you to join us on the second leg of our trip."

Staring at Mr. Barnes, Mia couldn't help but admire the smooth way he'd laid it all out for her. He'd been gracious as well as clear and concise with the information. Their whole group had delayed their departure to help her, and what had she done? She'd asked him a very personal question without even stopping to consider how easily he might bar her from boarding and using their kinky cruise as a way to escape the hounds of hell nipping at her heels.

Instead of being insulted by her impertinence, he'd

leaned his head back and laughed before continuing on as if she hadn't asked about his personal sex life. The stunned looks on Brock and Tucker's faces told her it wasn't the reaction they'd expected either. *Dandy.* Before she could think up a lame excuse for her inexcusable behavior, he'd held up his hand to silence her. The man was obviously used to being obeyed, and for the first time, his earlier words began to sink in.

"Aha. I see you've finally thought of something else you probably should have asked about first, haven't you, sweet Mia?" He turned to Brock and grinned, "I do so love that look of dawning realization on a sub's face. That moment when their eyes are opened for the first time to something completely unexpected. Come."

He held out his arm again, and she slid her hand back into the bend of his elbow as she'd been trained to do since she was old enough to walk. One of the advantages of having grown up in her grandfather's home was being taught how to behave properly in a wide variety of social situations. Mia knew how to properly enter a ballroom, where to sit to best be *seen* at a charity function, and how to introduce any dignitary you could imagine, so the move was reflexive on her part.

A noise behind her almost caused her to lose a step as they made their way up the gangway. *Did Brock just growl at me?*

Cameron Barnes patted her hand and whispered, "Don't turn sweet girl. Let them stew a bit, it will do them good and add to your first play experience."

Play experience? Oh, brother.

CAM COULDN'T REMEMBER the last time he'd enjoyed a sudden change in plans as he had this one. Seeing old friends was always a pleasure, but seeing them completely derailed by a woman who appeared blissfully unaware of the power she held over them held more entertainment potential than he'd imagined possible. But then again, maybe the two Deitz brothers needed a refresher course as Masters. He'd watch them and intercede if it became necessary.

Ten minutes later, the introductions had been made, and he looked on as Carl escorted CeCe and Mia to one of the freight elevators reserved for the crew. Cam was pleased to see the instant rapport between the women; his lovely pet had far too few friends since they'd moved to St. Maarten. She'd become socially isolated, and he and Carl had been mulling over various solutions for several months.

Cam was considering moving back to Houston—at least part-time—because Cecelia was no longer able to hide the loneliness he suspected she'd been struggling with long before Carl brought it to his attention. Once she was pregnant again, the feeling would be magnified because his lovely wife did nothing by half-measure, and she'd fall head first into the hormone whirlpool of pregnancy. Yes, it was definitely time to set the plans to move in motion.

"Follow me. I've set up a temporary control center for this operation apart from the one we were using for security and everyday club safety." In minutes they were standing in a room filled with monitors and state-of-the-art communication equipment. There wasn't anyplace on the ship or its perimeter they couldn't see with a few strokes to the keyboard, and thanks to real-time satellite imagery, they'd also be able to see anyone approaching miles before they would ordinarily appear on the horizon.

"Jesus, man. Were you planning on running an op?" Tucker's observation wasn't unreasonable—all things considered.

"Are you telling me you just happened to bring along the extra equipment to set this up? Fuck, you don't travel light, do you, Cam?" Brock's assessment was more accurate than he knew, but Cam never took the safety of his family for granted.

His home in St. Maarten was a virtual fortress, just as his penthouse apartment in Houston had been. Finding a new home in Texas that would allow his family the same level of security wasn't going to be easy. He had no problem remodeling, but patience wasn't his best trait.

"Given my background and contacts, security breaches are always a possibility. I find it easier to be prepared." Grinning, he added, "We'll have three semi-trucks waiting at the dock to off-load when we arrive in Houston if that tells you anything."

Brock and Tucker both shook their heads in amazement.

"For the record, my wife doesn't know this room exists. Ordinarily, I wouldn't keep safety concerns a secret, but this trip was a gift to her, so I'd prefer to keep her out of the loop, for now." If they'd been on land, he'd have sat down with CeCe and given her more information, but being surrounded by the azure colored water of the southern Caribbean afforded him more flexibility. There wasn't any reason to spoil her vacation unless he was forced to.

Turning to the other men, Cam leveled them with a look he knew they'd understand as a required shift in their conversation.

"Is she going to be able to pull this off? Does she have any experience in the lifestyle other than the very interesting content on her e-reader?" Tucker's brows arched in surprise, and Brock's grin was filled with the devil's delight. Cam shrugged as he added, "You have to love a woman who diligently backs up her devices." It had been far too easy to access her online files. Someone needed to have a chat with her about the importance of secure passwords.

"We haven't talked to her about what's going to be expected of her because we didn't really know what level of play would be taking place." Cam wanted to roll his eyes at Brock's bullshit answer.

"Very well, let me refresh your memories. I started a club in Houston where edge play was acceptable and common. I trained sexual Dominants who were expected to be able to provide whatever level of play their submissives needed."

"Fucking smart ass," Tucker's muttered curse made Cam grin.

"Listen, you'll have tonight to walk around and get a feel for what she's comfortable with and how you can best meet those needs. No one will question you wanting to gauge the group dynamics your first night on board, but after that, you'll need to participate in order to maintain your cover." Brock nodded, but Cam noted the way Tucker's mouth thinned into a tight line.

"Do any of your guests have communication access to the outside world?"

"Not now. We're jamming signals until we're out-of-range of land, then we'll be okay until our next port of call in Mexico." He hoped his friends had established themselves as a menage by then, so no one gave them a second thought during their time in Cozumel. He wasn't looking forward to the stop and would skip it if possible, but Cam knew several of their younger guests were looking forward to the street party atmosphere and water activities readily available in the area.

"If you haven't won everyone over before then, we'll need to reassess. I don't want to do that because the more twists you put in the plot, the more difficult the story is to keep straight. And for obvious reasons, this isn't going to have my undivided attention gentlemen, so you need to make it work with as little fanfare as possible." When both men nodded, Cam slid a file across the counter and flipped it open.

"Here's what I've gotten from Prairie Winds so far. There is something suspicious about the situation with the grandfather. I can't put my finger on it, but something isn't right with his security detail. Mendez is genuinely concerned about his granddaughter, but his chief of security isn't playing from the same sheet of music."

"What the fuck?" Cam wasn't sure if Brock's question came as a result of what he'd said or what the other man had read in the latest memo from Kyle West. When he slid the printout to Tucker, Cam had his answer.

"We'll need clothes. None of the stuff in our bags is going to pass as club-wear. We're going to be asking Mia some serious questions, but I have a feeling we'll hit a brick wall until we send her over a few times and slip past the barriers I'm sure she's erected."

Cam was relieved the men shared his suspicions because if they were right, retired general Joseph Moreno had more reason to make sure Mia didn't return than he did to bring her home safely. And if they were right, the man on the inside might prove to be their more formidable adversary.

"We'll upload the contents of her electronics to Prairie Winds and see if they can pull any additional information. When I talked to Koi earlier today, he was strung pretty tight." What else could he say about the man he'd mentored and considered one of his most gifted protegees? The man was fighting hard, wanting to fly to Columbia himself. It had taken Cam almost an hour to talk him out of the plan.

"He needs to stay with Dr. Tyson. If the men holding her husband are looking for something specific, leaving her unprotected would be the worst possible scenario," Brock nodded in agreement. There were too many unanswered questions and it was entirely possible Tally would be targeted as well.

Chapter Five

MIA LIKED CECE Barnes immediately. Their rapport was effortless, and Mia felt like a giant weight had been lifted from her chest as the two of them were escorted to the elevator. Perhaps she'd made a mistake isolating herself even after moving from her grandfather's estate. She'd never had the opportunity to make friends, so it had seemed natural to keep to herself. Sure, she talked to the people she worked with when on location shoots, but outside of the upper echelon social group who surrounded her family, Mia didn't really know many people other than a few colleagues.

Carl Phillips kept pace with them without making any effort to intrude on their conversation. She noticed Carl maintained a physical connection with CeCe at all times, and she couldn't help but wonder about the dynamics of their relationship. *How did CeCe manage to keep two Doms happy? Did she spend equal amounts of time with each man? How on Earth did she keep track? Was jealousy ever an issue? How did she explain Carl's presence to those outside their lifestyle?* She was looking forward to seeing the three of them interact for longer than a couple of minutes as she had during introductions.

Her insatiable curiosity was one of the things that had always gotten her into trouble. It had also been responsible for a very unpleasant encounter with one of her grandpapa's most trusted employees. Dammit, if she hadn't been such a freaking snoop, she'd have never stumbled on his little side business. He'd been asking her to dinner for months, but there was something about him that set her on edge, so she'd always politely declined.

CeCe's delighted giggle surprised Mia and thankfully, pulled her back to the moment. She turned to the other woman as the doors of the elevator slid closed and smiled when she saw the mischief dancing in her eyes.

"I can practically hear the gears spinning in your head. Please feel free to ask me anything... I promise I won't be offended by your questions, and I'll answer as honestly as I can." Her eyes flickered to the man standing beside her, a sly smile curving up the corners of her mouth. "And Carl is good at keeping a confidence unless it involves my safety... then all bets are off."

Carl's eyes warmed, soft laugh lines etching at their corners as he looked down at the woman he was obviously in love with.

"You'll be honest, but as discrete as a physician can be."

CeCe's giggle was contagious when she turned to Mia and rolled her eyes. "My husbands are not always pleased with what they call my doctor-attitude when it comes to anything related to the body."

Mia watched as the muscles under Carl's jaw tightened, and his shoulders seemed to tense beneath the black shirt he wore like a second skin.

"I've spent my entire career speaking openly about the human body, and that's not going to change... no matter how many times I end up over their laps or a spanking bench for what they consider my indiscrete remarks."

Mia wanted to laugh out loud at the look on Carl's face, but she managed to tamp down her amusement until he subtly shifted, one foot to the other. His reflection in the shiny surface of the elevator clearly showed the outline of his impressive erection, and she realized he'd been trying to relieve the pressure as his cock pressed against his zipper. Unable to hold back any longer, Mia's giggle bubbled up before she could stop it, and CeCe quickly followed suit.

Both women were wiping tears from their eyes as they walked off the elevator, and Carl turned them toward the ship's small salon. She heard him mutter a curse about Cam owing him as they stepped inside a room that reminded Mia of the lush rainforests in the Columbian mountains. Of course, smooth marble countertops were a vast improvement over the rock ledges near her favorite waterfall and avoiding being sliced by palm leaves as she'd made her way into the spa's sweet smelling lobby was also a plus. Hell, it was a better deal all the way around.

Carl spun CeCe around in a move so smooth, Mia had to smile. *I'll bet he's quite the dancer.* CeCe's eyes widened, but they were filled with love rather than surprise, and Mia felt a pang of jealousy when she saw the familiarity in her new friend's eyes. This was a move they'd done many times. Their love was easy, and she admired their obvious comfort in one another's company.

"I'm leaving you here, but I'll be close by if you need me, baby." Mia felt like an interloper eavesdropping on their private moment. Carl's blonde hair and blue eyes were a sharp contrast to CeCe's dark hair and eyes as he leaned down to kiss her goodbye.

"They aren't going to let you drive the boat are they?" CeCe giggled at her own question, and Carl gave her ass a sharp swat, making her squeak. Turning to Mia, CeCe grinned. "I love him with all my heart, but his driving terrifies me. I keep saying he missed his calling as a stunt driver."

"You're being awfully brave for a woman who has a date with a flogger this evening. Might want to check the sass, baby." Carl slid his hands under the short dress his wife was wearing and palmed her ass, making no attempt to cover her bare flesh as he kneaded the soft globes. For her part, CeCe was lost in his kiss and appeared completely at ease having her backside flashed for all to see.

Mia felt her cheeks heat in embarrassment, but she still couldn't tear her gaze from the scene taking place right in front of her. Carl gave CeCe's exposed rear one last swat before turning his attention to the woman who'd stepped from behind a wall of tropical plants.

"Take care of these ladies, and I'll remind you that Mr. Barnes' instructions take precedence over any objections they might raise." Leveling a look at Mia, then CeCe, he turned back to the exotic beauty Mia assumed was one of the estheticians and added, "If either of them gives you any problem, give me a call, and I'll make them walk the plank."

The implied threat didn't seem to alarm CeCe, but it sent a shiver of something between fear and anticipation up Mia's spine. She had no desire to get thrown overboard, but a sudden flash of herself at Brock and Tucker's mercy set off a wave of heat that made her pussy throb.

As soon as the door snicked shut behind Carl, the technician ushered them to the back. Mia almost cried with relief when she saw drinks and sandwiches set out in a beautiful array.

"Come on, I know you have to be hungry after traveling for so many hours. And we'd better drink up, too. The look Carl gave us doesn't bode well for our pink bits."

"Excuse me?" Mia had only been partially paying attention, distracted as she piled her small plate with finger sandwiches and fruit. "Pink bits?"

"Yes, indeed. My Masters have a thing for smooth skin... everywhere. If they set up this up, you can be sure there will be wax involved... and your esthetician is about to see parts of you only your gynecologist sees on a regular basis." The petite brunette stopped and looked up as if lost in thought for a few seconds before a cat-that-ate-the-canary smile spread across her face. "Come to think of it, I think the staff at Dark Desires Spa sees my hoo-ha more often than my OB or gyno. Damn, that probably says a lot about my lifestyle, doesn't it?"

"Wax?" *Oh, fudge.*

Two hours later, Mia was grateful for the alcohol she'd had before her waxing session started. Having hot wax smeared on her mound had been embarrassing enough, but when the sadist wielding the wax covered stick told her to put her legs in the table's stirrups, Mia found out quickly CeCe hadn't been kidding about the two of them becoming intimately acquainted. Having the hair surrounding her pussy yanked out by the roots had been painful, but when the woman smeared the heated mix around her anus, Mia started to panic.

"No need to worry, we do this treatment all the time. You'll love how sensitive you are to all forms of anal stimulation and penetration."

Oh dear Lord in heaven, please tell me this young woman isn't cheerleading the virtues of a bald ass. One thing for sure... none of the erotic romance books she'd read had adequately prepared her for the humiliation of being spread eagle with her feet in the air while a stranger used a popsicle stick to smear citrus scented wax around her anus. She wondered which was more painful... the embarrassment or the waxing itself when the first strip was unceremoniously yanked from her rear entrance, making her rehearse every foul word in her vocabulary... *twice!* Decision made... the waxing was definitely more painful.

"Damn, Mia," CeCe's voice sounded from the other side of the curtain dividing their cubicles, "I don't think I've ever heard anyone make that particular sound before." It was easy to hear the laughter in her new friend's voice before she let out a startled screech of her own. "Holy fucking... Hail Mary full of grace. Give a girl a little warning next time." Mia started to ask about the strange glow coming from the other side of the cloth divider when CeCe sighed.

"I'm glad I finally let my Masters talk me into laser treatments. Before long, I won't have to worry about stubble or waxing... I'll be billiard ball smooth for the rest of my life. That ought to give my geriatric nurses something to chatter about someday."

"Pet, I think your reputation alone will give them enough ammunition for years. Now be a good girl and let the technicians work. I have big plans for you."

Mia recognized Cameron Barnes voice, and she started to panic at the thought of him being so close when she was completely exposed. When she started struggling to sit up, warm hands gripped her shoulders and held her in place.

"Stay where you are, Kodak." Mia looked up into Tucker's sea green eyes, torn between being mortified to find him standing over her and enthralled by his penetrative gaze. To the man's credit, he didn't take his eyes from hers, and she breathed a sigh of relief when she remembered the privacy screen the technician had draped over a rod suspended from the ceiling.

"Kodak?" Her voice sounded husky even to her own

ears, and the gleam in his eyes let her know he hadn't missed the heat she'd failed to conceal.

"You're a photojournalist. It seems fitting, and I won't have to worry about any other submissive responding to your nickname when we're in the club."

"Club?"

He chuckled, and she almost rolled her eyes when she realized she sounded like an ignorant doof echoing his words back to him.

"Yes, the club. We're just doing a walk through tonight for a couple of reasons. First, you've had too much to drink to negotiate a real scene although I'm not opposed to playing a bit. And second, we need to learn more about what appeals to you before we play in public."

She felt her body respond just before the last strip was pulled free, and she bit her lip to keep from cursing a blue streak. Tucker smiled, and she sucked in a breath at the way the high voltage gesture totally transformed his appearance. Gone was the grim soldier, and in his place was a man so gorgeous, he looked more like an air-brushed photo from a high-end fashion magazine.

"Yes, you've certainly had too much to drink to play safely, at least until you've eaten, sweet cheeks. But I'm looking forward to seeing that dazed look in your eyes again, very soon." He shocked her by leaning down and pressing a chaste kiss to her lips. "Cam and I were just doing a walkthrough of the ship and decided to check on you ladies. I'll see you in a bit. Behave." He kissed her once more before disappearing as quickly as he'd appeared.

For several seconds Mia lay perfectly still as she battled the alcohol-induced brain fog and tried to decide whether or not his visit had been real or a figment of her over-active imagination. By the time the staff helped her to her feet, she'd chalked it up to a very hot, tequila and wine induced fantasy. What the hell had she been thinking switching to shots after the wine CeCe had sworn would take the edge off her nervousness? The booze on top of stress-induced fatigue had her weaving on her feet.

"Hey, CeCe, is the room spinning on your side of the curtain?"

"Nope, but the plants are dancing a jig. I don't know whether I should mention that to my Masters or not. On the one hand, it might be a security issue, but it might be the wine, and it seems um... well, not so... shit. I think they might not believe me if I said the palms were living it up."

"Pet, what am I going to do with you? How many glasses of wine did you have?" Cameron Barnes' voice sounded from the door as the curtain between the cubicles slid open. He stood with his feet spread apart, arms crossed over his chest looking like a pirate... except he didn't have on breeches... or a wooden leg... or a parrot... or a hat. *Okay, maybe not exactly like a pirate.*

Mia started giggling at her own absurdity, and before she knew it, she was laughing so hard, she stumbled, falling against a wall of warm male perfection. Brock Deitz's arms encircled her, and she breathed in the scent of freshly showered masculinity. A rumble against her cheek was followed by him pulling back just enough to look down at her.

"Careful, baby." Brock seemed to be studying her, but it was hard to tell with him weaving around so much.

"Hey, CeCe, your dancing palms have nothing on Brock. He's dancing too, but I don't think his feet are moving." She thought he rolled his eyes, but it was hard to tell with him swaying back and forth like a willow in the wind.

"Shhh. Geez, Mia. You don't give Doms that sort of ammo… it always comes back to paddle your ass. Damn, didn't you listen to anything I said? Wait. We didn't talk about *that stuff*, did we? Hell's bells, all I told you was how hot the sex was. Okay, survival skills class is tomorrow." CeCe's giggle was contagious, and Mia didn't even try to hold back her own.

"Christ. You're toasted, sweetheart. And you didn't even have that much to drink."

"How do you know? And I did. Have a lot, I mean. Well, a lot for me. I'm a lightweight with alcohol. Never built up any tolerance. Damned bodyguards, anyway. They were real wet-blankets when I was a teenager and in college. Don't do this. Don't do that. You can't drink that. Here have a glass of water, it's good for you. Blah, blah, blah. It was like having a whole bunch of nagging nannies following you around all the time." Squinting her eyes as she stared at Brock, pressing her palm to his chest, hoping it would still his swaying. "You aren't going to do that are you? Because that might be a deal breaker. How far are we from shore? Probably too far to swim, huh? Damn. I hate it when that happens."

When she felt his chest vibrating with laughter, she frowned. "It's not nice to laugh at people who are cognitively impaired, you know. Aren't Americans really keen on being politically correct and all that?" She wasn't sure she'd been able to disguise her hurt feelings with indignation, but she'd certainly tried.

"Doms are exempt from PCBS, sweetheart. And cognitive impairment at your own hand also means you are outside those protective parameters." Brock's voice was filled with amusement, but it was impossible to be angry when she was struggling to make sense of what he'd said. Seemed a lot of politically correct bull shit to say he didn't believe in PCBS, but she wasn't certain enough to argue the point.

"I'm hungry." She slapped her hand over her mouth and flinched when it stung. *Damn. I can't believe I did that or that I blurted that out. How rude.* Her grandmother would spin herself out of her grave if she heard Mia say something so blunt. Her grandmama's sweet voice moved through her mind like a sweet memory. *"You never ask your host for anything except the ladies room, dear, it's so very common to ask for more."* She'd been in her early teens when her grandmother died, but she'd never forgotten the lessons she'd taught.

"No, sweetheart," Brock shook his head, "it's not rude to tell your Dom you are hungry. My brother and I expect you to tell us what you need." When his hand cupped the side of her face, she instinctively pressed closer enjoying the warmth of his touch. "Now, let's get you dressed, and we'll have a bite to eat before we get on with our evening."

Chapter Six

BROCK KNEW HE was fighting a losing battle to hold back his laughter, but Mia was the cutest drunk he'd ever seen. She was damned lucky he'd been the one to pick her up from the spa rather than Tucker. His brother would have taken exception to her complete lack of awareness of her surroundings. Hell, she'd stood in front of him without a stitch of clothing and never blinked. He'd enjoyed the view, but he was certain things would have been much different if she'd been sober. Pulling a sheet from the table, he wrapped it around her and led her down the short hall.

"Where are we going? I can't walk around the ship dressed in a sheet, people will think I lost my clothes."

"Do you know where your clothes are, baby?" Brock heard the amusement in his own voice and grinned at the wrinkle between her furrowed brows.

"Well... not exactly."

"Then it seems you have lost your clothes, so anyone making that assumption would be right."

"That doesn't mean I want to advertise how inept I am when I have a shot or three of tequila." She surprised him by stopping and tugging on the front of his shirt until he leaned down close enough for her to whisper, "This boat is full of Doms and subs, you know."

Pulling back, he gave her what he hoped was a genuinely surprised look. Nodding, she added, "It's true. CeCe told me about it. She has two husbands." When she held up three fingers, he gently tucked one of the slender digits back down. "Oops. Thanks. Anyway, I thought that only happened in my books, but CeCe said she knows lots of women who have two husbands. Do you think that's true? Because if it is that would be hot."

The sense of satisfaction that moved through him was probably more intense than it should have been, but for once he wasn't leading with logic. Giving her a quick kiss, he grinned.

"It's true and you're right, it's very hot. Come on, we've got a quick stop to make before we go upstairs to eat." Moving the short distance to the boutique, he led her in and pointed to the array of dresses set out for her. "Which of these would you like to wear this evening?"

Brock knew she was no stranger to nice clothing, so he was surprised to see the unmistakable sheen of tears in her pretty blue eyes. Her family's wealth and social position would have exposed her to any number of situations requiring dresses far more expensive than what he'd chosen, so her reaction surprised him. The file Micah forwarded was filled with pictures of her dressed in designer dresses he knew had to have cost thousands of dollars. Standing back watching her rub the fabric of several dresses between her fingers, he wondered at her emotional reaction to the most conservative selections they'd had in her petite size.

"These are so pretty, but they might be a bit skimpy for someone my size." *Her size? What the hell?* "I'm flattered you think these would look nice on me, but I don't think anyone will want to see this much… well, this much of me."

A soft whoosh of air behind him signaled Tucker's arrival, and Brock smiled to himself. *Sweetheart, you should have chosen while you had the chance.*

TUCKER HAD BEEN watching the security feed upstairs, so he already knew what was taking so long, but that didn't stop him asking when he saw Brock and Mia standing in the small dress shop. "What's the hold up?"

Knowing his brother, he'd given her a choice, which of course would explain the delay. What he hadn't expected was the genuine smile that spread across her heart-shaped face when she saw him.

"Oh, look at the pretty dresses, Tucker. Did you help Brock pick these out? I've never had a man pick out a dress for me. These are lovely, but I think I'd better look around and find something that will cover a bit more of my ass… ets."

Tucker crossed his arms over his chest and glared at her. "Valliant attempt to save your ass… ets, but too little and far too late."

"I think the alcohol is keeping our sub from firing on all cylinders, brother," Brock chuckled at her confused look. "Seems she has an incredibly low tolerance—something we'll have to keep a careful watch on."

"Indeed," Tuck's blunt response might have been directed at his brother, but he didn't take his eyes off the beauty standing in front of him. The white cotton sheet she was draped in clearly outlined the dark rose areolas that were fast becoming tight peaks, reaching out as if seeking his attention. Quickly scanning the three dresses Brock had selected, he grasped the one in the center. He bet the deep sapphire would match her eyes when they darkened with desire. Lifting the hanger off the hook, he returned his attention to Mia.

"Drop the sheet, Kodak."

To her credit, she only hesitated for an instant before her hands moved to the knot between her breasts. The booze still clouded her eyes, but she met his challenge without flinching or letting her gaze drop from his. With the sheet pooled around her feet, she was breathtakingly beautiful.

"You are gorgeous, sweet cheeks. I can hardly wait to see if I'm right about this color." Gathering the fabric in his hands, he smiled. "Arms up." When the dress settled over her, he nodded his approval but noticed her frown.

"It barely covers my backside. And I need underwear. If I bend over or reach for anything, I'm going to flash everyone." Tucker had seen the contents of her e-reader, so the flicker of recognition in her eyes told him she wasn't ignorant to the rules of a D/s relationship. If this was a test, he was more than up to the challenge. *Bring it, sweet cheeks.*

"Baby, every passenger on this ship is either a sexual Dominant or a submissive. I assure you, they will be far more shocked if you *are* wearing panties than they'll be seeing that lovely ass and smooth pussy." Brock was right, but Tuck wasn't sure Mia was convinced they were committed to the roles they'd already outlined. Hell, the alcohol had probably negated a lot of what they'd outlined earlier.

"No panties. We aren't doing a scene tonight, but I reserve the right to check your responses to what you're seeing as we walk around. No one will believe we are your Doms if we let you wear more than this." He waved his hand at her dress. The fact was she would probably be covered far more than any of the other subs—something he was looking forward to remedying soon enough.

"We'll have our hands on you, Kodak, you can take that to your grandfather's bank." *And we've already warned you, we will begin as we intend to go.* He might not intend to have a long-term relationship with her, but he damned well planned to enjoy the benefits of their arrangement for the short time it would last. He'd always prided himself on being honest—with himself as well as with others, and there was a nagging voice in the back of his mind taunting him that he'd just told himself the mother of all lies.

Tucker watched as she chewed on her lower lip, her eyes searching the room as if a solution was going to magically appear in the small space. He could practically hear her mind whirling as she decided whether this was a battle worth fighting. When she looked to Brock for help, Tucker almost laughed out loud. Why did women always think his brother was the softer touch? While it was true, Brock was more inclined to use charm to persuade a sub, but he had a palm the size of a bear's paw that could light a sub's ass on fire. And in the end, they were both dominant to the bone.

"Those pretty pleading eyes won't work on me baby," Brock shook his head. "Your safety is too important."

"She's read enough about the lifestyle to know the rules, haven't you sweet cheeks?" Tucker snorted a laugh when she leveled a glare in his direction. "Interesting reading list on your e-reader, Kodak. Very interesting, indeed. And while I don't advocate fiction reading as an alternative to real-life experience, it certainly goes a long way to introduce the topic." He closed the distance between them with two purposeful steps.

"We'll add that glare to your growing list of offenses. Don't think for a moment that look will be ignored if it takes place in public. Don't force our hands, Mia. I'd rather our first public scene was negotiated ahead of time, and I think we'll all enjoy it much more if it's about pleasure rather than punishment."

"You're right." Mia surprised him when she nodded. "I'm sorry, that was disrespectful. Fruit salad, my grandmother would have batted me on the back of my head for that." Tucker blinked at her wondering what the hell fruit salad had to do with her grandmother. Waving her hand as if dismissing the obvious question in his eyes, she added, "Lucia Mendez was a lot of things, but tolerant of foul language and disrespect were not at the top of the list. I learned at an early age to use everyday words that clearly did not fit into the conversation to express myself when my friends would have interjected profanity. Much easier than getting smacked."

"It sounds like your grandmother was a wonderful woman, and we'll look forward to hearing your creative substitutions for cursing. But right now, I'm hungry and you need to eat something to counteract the tequila and wine." Tucker smoothed his palm from her shoulder to wrist.

Mia's entire face lit up, and she excitedly asked, "You have tequila? CeCe and I had tequila shots at the spa, but someone must have complained because all of a sudden, we couldn't have anymore. CeCe said the walls have eyes and ears. Do you think that's true? It's kind of creepy if you ask me. I thought Americans were all about protecting privacy and all that?"

Tucker stared at her in open-mouthed astonishment as his brother cackled with laughter. Shaking his head, Tuck encircled her delicate wrist with his large hand and led her out of the boutique.

Fighting his attraction to Mia was going to be a battle of epic proportions. There was a part of him that wanted to sweep all his reservations to the side and embrace the opportunity to spend uncensored time enjoying a woman's company for the first time in over a year. The struggle to remain distant hadn't been difficult until now, but it was easy to see the effort required was going to be exhausting with the dark-haired beauty beside him.

Glancing at Brock, Tucker wanted to roll his eyes at his brother's satisfied expression. *There will be no living with him now. If it doesn't work out, he'll blame me. If by some star-crossed miracle it does, he'll never stop reminding me he was right.*

Chapter Seven

MIA WAS CERTAIN they'd stepped into another world as soon as her bare feet crossed the threshold of the motion-activated doors of the ship's main deck. Stars danced against the black velvet sky, and she sucked in a breath at the beautiful picture.

"It simply steals your breath, doesn't it, Kodak?"

When she realized her feet had stopped moving, she looked up at Tucker and smiled. "The night sky is always the best show around, but it's even more spectacular on the water. Without city lights or the cover of trees, you get a real sense of how truly vast and remarkable it is. It makes me feel both insignificant and important at the same time." Tucker's brow furrowed, and she understood his confusion.

"There is so much out there... it's unimaginable how much we don't know. But at the same time, I feel important because in all the vast array, I'm here, and I can have an impact. Knowing I can affect the vibration of this universe which in turn sets off a chain reaction touching others... well, that makes me rethink everything I say and do. I want to make sure the energy I send out is as positive as possible."

"That's beautiful, baby," Brock's arms came around her from behind, and he pulled her back against his chest, "and one of the most unselfish things I've ever heard anyone say."

His words warmed her and chased away the cool breeze circling the deck, but she had the feeling Brock's comment had been intended as much for Tucker as they'd been for her. Mia's questions about that would have to wait because Tucker gave her a quick tug out of Brock's embrace and resumed walking.

Cursing her short legs, Mia was suddenly grateful she was barefoot, especially when she looked around to see the killer heels most of the women were wearing. *Thank you, guardian angels, for not letting them put me in shoes like those.* She'd barely made it down the grand staircase in her grandfather's mansion for her quinceanera, and the kitten heels she'd worn had paled in comparison to what she was seeing now. Her sweet sixteen party had been one of the worst nights of her life. The entire process had felt more like a first showing at an auction than a coming of age celebration.

When she tripped in her rush to stay abreast of the Deitz brothers, Brock groused at his brother.

"Slow down, asshole. Damn, she's going to get hurt just trying to keep up. Christ, I'm hungry, too, but there's no need to race."

Tucker slowed before pulling open the door to the restaurant. They were seated immediately, the maître d' giving them a knowing smile when the men pointed to a corner booth, then slid in on either side of her.

Their thighs pressed the full length of her own, warming her bare skin. When their hands settled over her knees, Mia let out a startled gasp. Tucker gave her a quick squeeze she thought was meant as reassurance, but instead, it sent electricity skittering all the way to her quickly dampening sex.

"Are you allergic to anything, Kodak?" Tucker's question took her by surprise, and she could only stare at him blankly. "Sweet cheeks, it's not a difficult question. We're getting ready to order and need to know if there is anything you can't eat." The amusement in his voice was vaguely annoying. Blast the man for knowing the effect he had on her.

Feeling like a fool for being confused by the question, she nodded. "Shellfish. I can't eat any of it. Unfortunately, I like shrimp much more than they like me." He gave her a quick smile before returning his attention to the menu. When she looked at Brock, she noted he was studying the wine list, and she couldn't hold back her groan. "I'm not usually a big wine drinker, but CeCe was very persuasive."

"I have known Dr. Cecelia Barnes for several years," Brock smiled, "so I'm fully aware of her charm. I'm not planning to order wine tonight, but I was interested in what was available. We never drink before we play, and in our line of work, alcohol is a dangerous distraction. I suspect you don't drink often either, or you wouldn't have been so affected by the small amount you had earlier this evening."

"What you couldn't see, Kodak, was CeCe throwing back two shots for every one you were having."

"What? You could hardly tell she'd been drinking... at least until the very end. Good Lord, you all probably think I'm a real amateur." Shaking her head, she was relieved when the waiter finally appeared with her water. She drained it quickly, setting the empty crystal goblet back on the table before Brock had finished ordering their dinner. The waiter gave her a cheeky grin and discreetly removed her glass to refill it.

By the time their food arrived, they'd asked her dozens

of questions about her work. She hadn't held anything back when they'd asked her about her sources, particularly those related to Senator Tyson.

"Remember, I didn't know who I was pursuing. I had no idea the American I kept hearing rumors about was a U.S. Senator. I only discovered his name when I searched the internet a few days after meeting him."

"Why did you chase the story if you didn't know who the man was?"

She understood Tucker's skepticism, but that didn't mean it didn't hurt to know he didn't really trust her.

"I'm not sure if I was chasing the story or running." She cursed herself for muttering the words out loud because even though they'd only been whispered, it was obvious from the shift in Brock and Tucker's body language they'd heard her. *There's no reason to make this more complicated than it is already, Mia.*

She'd had been planning to slip out of the country for over a year. If she was going to take her career to the next level, she needed to be able to travel, but her grandfather's security team regularly thwarted her plans. She knew her grandfather well enough to recognize his logic. If he made it difficult enough, he hoped she'd give up and accept a position at the bank. What he'd never understood was her creative spirit would wither and die in that environment. She often wondered if her grandfather understood there was a line between protecting and smothering, and both of those concepts were on an entirely different sheet of music from controlling.

Shaking herself out of the melancholy threatening to swamp her, Mia explained, "I sent the pictures because he'd used what little energy he had to give me the pieces of the puzzle." When they didn't respond, she added, "I felt like he just wanted someone to know who he was or maybe those were the only fragments he'd been able to retain... I'm not really sure. But if it was important enough for him to drain the last bits of his reserves to tell me..." she let her words trail off because they didn't sound as convincing now as the emotion had felt when Senator Tyson's dazed eyes had met hers.

"Have you spoken with his wife?" Mia asked, pulling herself back from the memory of Karl Tyson's lost expression. "I've been worried I completely disrupted her life, but I didn't feel like it was fair to withhold the information." It was true. She hadn't wanted to hurt the other woman, but she didn't know who else to contact. And she darned well didn't trust the government... Columbian or United States. Mia had taken pictures for several exposés on government corruption and been shocked by how pervasive it was. Even worse was the discovery that the seedy sides of multiple governments were almost always linked to others through underhanded dealings.

The sudden realization she hadn't even considered the possibility Brock and Tucker were working for the United States government sent a white-hot bolt of fear through her. Mia couldn't believe she'd been so careless to blindly trust two men who were obviously well-trained soldiers. A wave of panic stole her breath, and all she could think about was escaping until she had time to find out who she was dealing with.

BROCK WATCHED HELPLESSLY as Mia's entire demeanor shift between one heartbeat and the next, and he had no idea what had triggered the change. The look of wild panic in her eyes baffled him. Nothing they'd discussed should have set her off. She shoved against him, then turned to Tucker before he saw her glance at the table. *Oh no, baby, you are not going to scamper under the table like a frightened rabbit.*

"Stop." He'd intentionally used a sharp tone, hoping to shock her back into focus. She froze in place giving him the few seconds he needed to grasp her upper arm and turn her until they were face to face. *Naturally submissive, aren't you baby?*

"Tell us what happened." Brock watched her eyes searching frantically around the room and knew he was losing her attention. "Eyes on me, pet. There's a good girl. Now, don't try to edit your answer, just tell us exactly what that was about."

"Who do you work for?" *What? Seriously?* Who the hell did she think they worked for?

"We are private contractors working for Kent and Kyle West's Prairie Winds team. We specialize in hostage rescues or any other mission that appeals to us."

Tucker turned her ever so slightly, using his fingers to tilt her chin until her eyes met his.

"We were Navy SEALs, Kodak, but we like being able to do the jobs we feel are important instead of doing Uncle Sam's dirty work." It was Tuck's explanation that had her letting out a deep breath and sagging like a wilting balloon. "Did you think we worked for the government, sweet cheeks?" When she nodded, Tucker grinned. "I've seen some of your work, Kodak, and I'd be willing to bet you don't have much faith in *any* government."

Brock watched as her eyes went wide before she sighed and nodded her head in reluctant agreement.

"No, I don't trust governments in general, and I don't think you should trust yours either, especially when it comes to Senator Tyson. All the rumors I heard indicated there were U.S. agents involved in his captivity. They have known all along he survived the plane crash."

Brock was stunned by her revelation, but it actually made perfect sense. He knew Kyle West suspected the CIA was, at the very least, aware of the rumors about a survivor. In Brock's opinion, the fact they hadn't investigated was reason enough to make them suspect.

KARL TYSON LEANED his shoulder against the warm tile of the shower wall and sent up silent prayers of thanks for the hot water sluicing over his body. After almost a year as a hostage, he hadn't thought he would ever be clean again. He may have traded one form of captivity for another, but at least this one came with a luxury suite. Karl appreciated the improvement in his surroundings, but what he didn't enjoy was the increasing number of hours each day he couldn't account for. His memory faded in and out, but the face of an angel with blonde hair and blue eyes was always the same when it floated through his dreams. In some dreams, she was smiling, but in others, she appeared frustrated or angry. And no matter how hard he tried, he hadn't been able to remember her name—hell, he wasn't even sure she was real.

Stepping from the shower, he dried himself and dressed in the clothes laid out for him. He wasn't sure which attendant was on duty today, but he hoped it was the woman. He couldn't remember her name, but she did a better job of ordering their food and didn't care what they watched on television. Before leaving the bathroom, he dropped to the floor and did ten push-ups. Not impressive, but certainly more than the one he managed the first day he'd arrived at the hotel. He wasn't sure why it felt so important, but something had compelled him to begin exercising his first day out of the chains he'd worn for a year.

There was another woman hovering in the dark fringes of his memory. This one had beautiful long dark hair and a camera, and she'd helped him escape from the jungle camp. Sometimes, late at night, her face faded in and out of his memory as he tried to remember what he'd said to her. Whatever it had been, the woman who'd unlocked the chain had been angry when he'd mentioned it later, insisting he'd been delusional, and no one else had helped them down the mountain. But the dark-haired beauty with the sparkling blue eyes still appeared in dreams along with the blonde angel.

Rubbing his forehead in agitation, Karl opened the door into the room and staggered at the realization he'd just remembered his name. His name was Karl. Karl Tyson. He blanked his expression when the man standing by the door frowned at him. Karl instinctively knew he couldn't let his hosts know his memory was slowly beginning to return.

Chapter Eight

MIA STOOD ROOTED in place, mesmerized by what she was seeing. She'd lost all track of time, watching the scene play out in front of her—she could have been standing here for hours for all she knew. Even the smallest glimpses were new wonders to explore, and she suddenly felt cheated by all her erotic romances. She'd believed the authors who had told her what it would be like, but this was so much... *more*.

The woman tied naked to the St. Andrew's cross was quivering, and Mia could hear her gasps each time the flogger fell. The skin over her upper back and ass was quickly morphing from flushed pink to a deep, blood red. Even at this distance, Mia could see the raised lines of welts, and the Dom periodically stopped to run his fingers over the marks. She couldn't see the man's face, but he was a sculpted work of art from the back, his muscles flexing beneath tanned skin shimmering with the sheen of perspiration. He'd pulled the black shirt off as they'd approached the stage. Even though he had yet to turn towards her, there was a niggling thought in the back of her mind... something about the fluidity of his movements seemed vaguely familiar.

The Dom wielding the leather strips was so focused on his submissive, he seemed oblivious to his growing audience. Even though she wondered if his face was a beautiful as his body, Mia couldn't take her eyes off his confident movements. Everything about him screamed dominance, and Mia knew instinctively this was a man completely enthralled with the woman in his care.

The woman whispered something Mia couldn't hear, but the Dom's reaction was immediate. He tossed the flogger aside and moved close enough to speak against her ear. Whatever he said sent a visible shiver through her entire being. Mia had never considered herself a voyeur but watching this couple's interaction was the most erotic thing she'd ever seen.

Intense focus radiated from the man whose black leather pants were so tight they looked like they'd been painted on as he pressed his bare chest against the woman's heated back. The soft leather molded to his body in a way that was probably illegal in many parts of the world. *Holy fucking hell.* His black leather boots looked well worn, telling her he spent plenty of time in this role. His arm snaked around the submissive's body, and Mia heard her soft pleading cry. A quick hand signal proceeded a click that sounded like a speaker being turned on, and the woman's panting cries filled the room.

"Master, please. I can't hold it back... Too good... Too much." What would it be like to feel a man's hands on her naked body? Petting, punishing, and proving himself worthy of her trust. How vulnerable would she feel being stripped and displayed for all to see? Was she capable of that level of submission? Mia's thoughts were spiraling out of control, and she swayed on her feet. Strong arms encircled her before her mind registered how precariously close she was to her knees folding out from under her.

"I've got you, baby."

Brock's simple words were enough to calm the emotional roller coaster she'd worried was going to drop her in an embarrassed heap. Mia hadn't been prepared for her vicarious response to the scene—the surge of adrenaline hyped her—but the circumstances didn't provide an outlet for the energy that followed. She continued to watch the scene, but Brock's embrace grounded her, and she suddenly felt safe despite her obvious vulnerability.

"Tell us what you see, Kodak. Use that photographer's eye that's made you so well known to describe it." Tucker's voice was deep and resonate, pulling her a little further back into the here and now. Mia appreciated him giving her something concrete to focus on.

"The first thing I noticed was the intensity of his concentration. Nothing seems to escape his attention. His focus on her seems unshakable." She didn't mention there was something familiar about him. It seemed crass to speak so personally about a man while being held by another.

Brock's fingers closed over her peaked nipples and gave them a sharp pinch. "Stop editing. We don't want you to tell us what you think we want to hear, we want the unvarnished truth. All of it."

"It isn't your responsibility to figure out what we want to hear. We'll never leave you wondering what we expect, sweet cheeks. And we'll reward honesty. Now, tell us what you saw that almost sent you ass over tea kettle."

STANDING TO THE side watching Mia's reaction to the flogging scene was the very definition of hot. Tucker wished he'd been close enough to hear the soft intakes of breath—the rapid rise of her chest with each fall of the flogger told him she was completely in the moment.

Damn, he wanted to hear the subtle moans he sensed were vibrating from deep in her chest. Mia had a sensual streak a mile wide and soul-deep, but Tucker would bet everything he owned she wasn't only new to the lifestyle, but sexually inexperienced as well.

When the three of them entered the room, CeCe had already been secured to the cross, and Cam had kept his back turned to the audience the entire time. Tucker didn't think Mia had made the connection between the Dom she was salivating over and the man she'd met earlier. He'd suppressed a groan when he realized Mia's gaze was glued to Cam rather than CeCe. In his experience, only the most natural submissives focused on the Dominant when watching a scene. Pleasing others was so deeply ingrained in their psyche, they zeroed in on the most dominant person in the scene. *It'll be interesting to see how she reacts when she realizes the man she's been drooling over is her new friend's husband.*

Even with a few feet separating them, Tucker could tell Mia's mind was getting in the way of her ability to connect with the way her body was responding to the scene. Tucker was grateful Brock had been close enough to catch her when she leaned precariously to one side. Brock raised a brow at Tucker, letting him know she'd almost dropped like a stone—that was something they'd need to watch closely.

Brock whispered words of reassurance, and Tucker saw her cheeks flush with what looked too much like embarrassment for his comfort. Hesitance and insecurity had no place in BDSM and not something he or Brock would allow. Stepping close enough he could feel the heat emanating from her, it was time to re-center her mind. Telling her to use her photographer's eye to describe what she was seeing seemed to give her some much-needed direction. Tucker kept his voice pitched so there was no doubt his words were a command, and he knew she'd sensed the difference. Her respiration stuttered, and her pupils dilated—yes, he'd hit the mark.

Her honest, but edited answers would have earned her a punishment if she belonged to them. For the first time, Tucker wished they weren't simply role-playing. Evidently, his brother was equally frustrated with her answer; he'd administered a quick admonishment that elicited a gasp from Mia and the air around them was suddenly filled with the musky scent of her arousal. *Just fucking great, like my cock needs any more reason to engorge against the zipper of these pants. At this rate, I'll never be rid of the metal imprint.*

Refocusing his attention on Mia, Tucker explained they expected her to not only be honest with them, but it was vital that she was honest with herself as well. Editing her answers proved she hadn't accepted herself in the way they'd demand. In Tucker's view, one of his most important jobs as a Dom was helping the submissive in his care reach her full potential. If she felt the need to hold back her deepest feelings, neither of them was going to succeed.

"It's not your responsibility to figure out what we want to hear. We'll never leave you wondering what we expect, sweet cheeks and we'll reward honesty. Now, tell us what you saw that almost sent you ass over tea kettle."

By the time she finished answering, Tucker was leisurely running his fingers through the soaked folds of her pussy. He'd stepped closer, blocking the view of the young

Dom on their right who was far more interested in Mia than he was in the woman on her knees with her lips locked around the guys flagging erection. The tears in the little sub's eyes said she hadn't missed her Dom's inattention either. *That jackass will probably be leaving the cruise alone.*

Smiling down at Mia, he softened his tone, "Good girl. Now, while we watch the rest of the scene, we're going to play a bit, but you'd best pay attention to the stage because we may well quiz you later." Tucker's voice held just enough of a teasing tone, he saw the corners of Mia's mouth turn up slightly before Brock gave her nipples another quick pinch.

"And remember, baby, you're not allowed to come until given permission. Stealing an orgasm is a serious offense, and we'd be forced to punish you." Brock paused as if weighing his words carefully when Tucker was certain the evil bastard knew exactly what he planned to say. *Fucking drama queen.* "Although I have to say, seeing you bent over grasping your dainty ankles baring that luscious ass right here in the middle of the room does hold a tremendous amount of appeal."

Brock's threat didn't fool Tucker. They'd already discussed that tonight was only about making sure Mia connected their touch with pleasure. One of them would make certain she was given the command to come before she spiraled out of control, but they would need to be on their toes since it was likely Cam had one hell of a finale planned.

The clanking of chains drew Mia's attention back to the stage, and Tucker grinned when her eyes widened in surprise at the cross's new position. CeCe was now laying almost flat on her stomach, her mouth and pussy the perfect height for what her Masters had planned. When a very naked and unquestionably aroused Carl Phillips stepped out of the shadows, recognition lit Mia's eyes, making her blush so deeply, Tucker could feel the heat radiating from her.

Cam's voice filled the room as he spoke to the woman spread out for everyone's viewing pleasure.

"Your pretty pussy is as ripe as a Georgia peach, Love. Everyone in the room is getting a good look at how much my naughty sub likes a good flogging. Now, pleasure your other Master with that wickedly talented mouth of yours, but don't make him come. Remember, all his tangy cum needs to shoot into your pussy if we're all going to be parents again."

"Their daughter is Cam's biological child," Brock whispered against Mia's ear, "but they've all decided this child should belong to Carl. Although I assure you, both men will consider the children their own."

"Aww. That's so sweet. I can't believe I didn't recognize them, so much for my photographer's eye."

Tucker knew her body was coming down from the arousal she'd felt earlier, but he wasn't sure if it was the conversation or her realization she'd been crushing on CeCe's husband. Mia didn't strike him as the type of woman who poached on her friends' men, but he'd been wrong before. Shaking off the melancholy threatening to steamroll him, Tucker yanked himself back to the present. Feathering his fingers through her slick folds, he leaned close to her ear.

"Your pussy is so slick, sweet cheeks. Did you enjoy the flogging?" She didn't answer immediately, but Tucker wouldn't punish her because he could see the glaze moving over her eyes as she watched Carl fuck CeCe's sweet mouth. When the other man's head fell back, and he groaned in pleasure loud enough to be heard across the room, Cam called for him to move to her pussy.

"Fuck her while I fuck you." Cam was already fisting his cock with lube. Learning Cameron Barnes had opened his relationship to a permanent third had been surprising enough because Cam was known for being a possessive bastard where CeCe was concerned. Learning there was a sexual relationship between the two men had left Tucker speechless. Discovering the two men had a shared history explained a lot, and Tucker knew Carl wasn't submissive to anyone but Cam. Tucker smiled to himself; he wasn't homophobic, he simply hadn't seen this twist in their story coming.

Carl pushed between the swollen petals of CeCe's pussy until he was balls deep, then went stock still.

"Fucking perfect, baby. You are scalding me. So fucking hot and tight."

The other man's words sent a rush of cream over Tucker's fingers, and he grinned at Brock over Mia's shoulder. Their little sub was a voyeur—good to know, and definitely valuable information they could use to their advantage.

Watching the trio on the stage, Tucker watched as Carl widened his stance and bent over CeCe, making room for Cam to step in behind him. They didn't have a clear view now, but it was easy to imagine what was happening by the groans of pleasure bouncing off every surface in the room.

Mia closed her eyes and relaxed back into Brock's embrace, exhibiting a level of comfort Tucker hoped she would eventually find with him as well. As if sensing his hesitance, her eyes fluttered open and instead of focusing on the scene, she locked her eyes on his and smiled.

"Thank you." The sincerity in her eyes made his heart melt despite his confusion about what she was thanking him for. "You've been so patient with me, your touch gentle but still igniting a fire in me that's been eye-opening, and I'm looking forward to learning more." Her voice had dropped so no one outside of their small circle could hear the words which would have easily given away the fact they hadn't spent any time together.

Their cover made accommodation for Mia being somewhat familiar with the lifestyle, but the three of them were supposed to have been together for only a few weeks. They'd be able to explain away some unfamiliarity, but they certainly needed to appear more comfortable with one another than they felt. So far, Tucker had been impressed with Mia's performance. She hadn't flinched when they'd touched her intimately, and he didn't know many women who could pull that off. But he also knew the real test was going to come when they played for the first time in one of the public areas tomorrow.

At Brock's nod, Tucker withdrew his fingers from her soaking sex and made a show of licking the sweet syrup from them.

"As always, you are sweet enough to make a man lose his mind for wanting to feast on you. I could spend hours licking your slick sex. Let's go, I want to see how your bare skin looks under the stars, Kodak." It was humbling to realize the words he'd spoken weren't about playing a part—they'd been spoken from the heart.

As they led her from the room, Tucker chuckled at CeCe's scream and the moans of both Cam and Carl as they found their own release. Mia stumbled in response, but he and Brock caught her between them easily.

"Easy, sweet cheeks. It's hot as hell knowing how affected you are watching the three of them."

Holding Mia tucked close against his side was no hardship. As petite as she was, it surprised him how perfectly she fit between them. The smug look on Brock's face made Tucker want to punch him, the arrogant bastard. Dammit, Tuck was going to have to be careful or his brother was going to push him into something he'd sworn he didn't want. The last thing he needed was to get his heart battered by a woman who would eventually return to Columbia. Shaking his head, Tucker reaffirmed his resolve to play but not get attached. *You can test drive without buying, you know.*

Chapter Nine

Koi leaned his hip against the kitchen counter as he studied the pensive woman across the room. Dr. Tally Tyson stood in front of the window, staring out into the moonlit backyard, but it was clear she wasn't seeing the vista laid out before her. She was lost in thought, oblivious to the way the rays of soft light danced over the snow-covered mountain peaks in the distance. He loved the view, and he knew if he lost her, he'd never see it the same way again. Having her to himself this past year had been a gift he hadn't done anything to deserve, but he hadn't had the strength to walk away. Hell, most of the time it had been a toss-up who'd needed the other one more.

Years of covert work had left its mark on him. He was emotionally distant and scarred. Before Tally, the only person he'd been able to fully trust was his sister, and for most of his career, he'd been forced to stay away from her as much as possible to ensure her safety. Knowing Kodi was now safely in the care of Taz and Nate Ledek eased some of the terror that had been his constant companion when he thought about how vulnerable she was.

Kodi loved with her whole heart and trusted everyone she met until they proved themselves unworthy—even then, she was too quick to forgive and forget, in his view. He would always be her big brother and probably wouldn't ever be able to fully relinquish the need to protect her, but it was getting easier to stand aside and let her husbands care for her.

Studying Tally's profile, he frowned when he noted the dark smudges under her eyes, proof she wasn't resting well. It frustrated him to think he'd slept like a fucking baby when she'd probably been lying awake wondering what the hell life was going to throw at her next. The packet of pictures she'd received had sent her reeling into a tailspin that seemed to be a recurring pattern lately. No one was surprised the pictures had upset her, but what the rest of the world didn't know was how torn she'd been by the revelation her husband was still alive.

Koi had seen it in her eyes and could hear it in the words she wasn't speaking, but no one else knew Tally to the depths of her soul like he did. Hell, Koi suspected he knew her better than Karl Tyson ever had. The man had been absent far more than he'd been present during their marriage, and they'd been on the brink of separating when Koi entered the picture.

He hated the guilt and indecision he could practically hear spinning through her thoughts. Koi suspected the only time she could set all the worries aside was when she was focusing on a patient during surgery. She'd work herself into an early grave if he didn't watch her. Sending her into sub-space would also do the trick, but he was treading carefully in that regard. He wanted her to associate his touch and dominance with pleasure rather than as a means of escape from emotional pain. Hell, that would make him little more than a fucking opioid addiction.

Koi had agreed to be Karl and Tally's *third*—an extra in their relationship, someone to enhance their sexual experiences and help look out for her when the good senator was in Washington rather than with his wife in

Montana. According to those who knew the couple well, the tension between them had been growing exponentially as Karl's career began skyrocketing and whispers of a future Presidential bid went from rumor to prediction.

Senator Tyson had needed his surgeon wife at his side in D.C. if he was going to make a legitimate bid as a candidate. She'd been adamantly opposed to moving back into a city filled with social circles bursting at the seams with venomous back-stabbing and rampant infidelity. Kodi had told him Tally hadn't believed there was any way her marriage would have survived. If she relented and moved back to Washington, she'd have certainly withered to the point divorce was her only option, leaving her stranded in a city she hated, without the career she loved. Or she could divorce him now, retain her sanity and career by staying in the state she'd adopted as her own.

When Karl's plane went down on a South American mountaintop, it appeared fate had made the decision for her. The search parties had taken days to reach the crash site, and what everyone had hoped would be a rescue was quickly reclassified as a recovery operation. Predators found the site before responders and from what his contacts had been able to learn, there hadn't been much left. Sharing those details with Tally had been one of the most difficult decisions he'd ever made, but he hadn't wanted to lie even if it was by omission. What kind of Dom would he be if he insisted on her transparency while holding back himself?

He'd spent many sleepless nights watching Tally vacillate between the relief she felt at not being forced to choose and the guilt that accompanied it. It had taken months for her to bounce back, and she'd only recently hit her stride and once again seemed genuinely happy. Of course, that was before the photos arrived and sent her spinning into the wind again. Koi hated seeing the uncertainty in her eyes when she considered the possibilities.

"There are only two reasons he hasn't let us know he's alive after he was rescued. Either he isn't allowed to, or he doesn't want to." And there it is, her whispered words confirming she'd drawn the same conclusion the rest of the team had come to before Koi and Tally returned to Montana. Most of the team leaned toward Stockholm Syndrome, but Koi had learned a long time ago not to make assumptions about politicians. In his experience, anyone with political aspirations was by definition, suspect.

Karl had been held in horrific conditions for almost an entire year, so any improvement would probably win him over quickly, and the potential that presented was sobering. As a beloved U.S. Senator, Karl would be a valuable ally if he returned to the Senate and took a sympathetic stand with the drug cartel. If he became President, his usefulness would be off the charts.

"Come here, *ma poupée*." *My little doll* had always been his pet name for Tally. He might use others during a scene or at the club, but the French phrase would always be his favorite since it was laced with affection. He was pleased when she turned and started walking to him immediately. No hesitation. She simply obeyed the command without letting her mind get in the way. Brilliant, loyal, submissive, and a heart-stopping beauty. Dr. Tally Tyson was about as perfect as any woman Koi had ever met, and no matter how hard he'd tried to fight it, he'd fallen in love with her the moment he'd seen her walking across the room at Mountain Mastery.

Karl had arranged the meeting, hoping Tally would agree to a third and Koi would be interested. Their chemistry had been electric, and it had blindsided him. Koi had done his homework—knew how gifted she was as a surgeon—and had seen her picture. But he'd been unprepared for how potent the whole package was, and he'd been leveled by the contrast between the lovely submissive and the fiery woman whose personality seemed larger than she was.

Pulling himself back from the memories, Koi shook his head at the detached look he saw in her eyes when she stopped in front of him. Pulling her into his embrace, he implored, "Talk to me, baby. I want to hear what's going through that brilliant mind of yours."

"I can't stop thinking about how adamant he was about the fact-finding trip everyone else believed was too dangerous. No one saw any potential for it yielding valuable information, yet he was almost obsessed with going. Karl refused to even entertain the idea of calling it off. When I first met him, I wrote that stubbornness off as tenacity. But, during that last year… as the scuttlebutt about him running for President picked up steam, it seemed more and more like a power trip." He felt the shudder that moved through her and tightened his hold. "We had a big fight about it, and I finally asked him if he was meeting another woman there."

Koi waited several long seconds for her to answer but her thoughts seemed to have drifted elsewhere, so he asked, "What did he say?"

"He scoffed at the question but didn't answer it. I've always wondered if I was right." The note of sadness in her voice made his heart squeeze. Koi knew better, but now wasn't the time for that discussion. He'd heard dozens of rumors since the plane crash linking Karl to any number of women and criminal organizations, but he discounted them as the usual D.C. drivel. For the first time, he wondered if he should tell Tally her sixth sense had been sadly accurate even if she had the information slightly askew.

Her body stiffened in his hold, and he set her back from him to have a clear view of her expressive face.

"What is it, *ma poupée*?" He could practically hear the wheels in her mind spinning as she mulled over something she hadn't yet spoken out loud.

"After the crash, I received Karl's life insurance payouts, immediately. The company we used for our personal policies paid just a couple of days after I received the check from his government policy. Neither of those companies waited for the official determination. Hell, the ink was barely dry on the newspaper articles about his death when those checks were cut." Koi raised a brow at her, quickly latching on to the track her thoughts were taking.

He'd seen the file and knew how substantial those payouts had been; most insurance carriers would have stalled as long as possible before issuing those checks. At the time, he'd been too busy caring for Tally to question it, but in hindsight, he had to agree with her—it was damned odd. Often, in such cases, the surviving spouse was assigned a government liaison to help them navigate the paperwork involved. Tally hadn't even needed an attorney because Uncle Sam had generously offered one of their own, free of charge—another abnormality.

"It seemed like a blessing at the time. I wasn't mired in one of the months-long battles I'd heard so many patients talk about when they lost their spouses. But now… in hindsight, it seems damned odd." He agreed, but he wanted her to talk it through, so he stayed silent. Tally might not be a Nobel Prize winner like Joelle Morgan, but her common-sense approach and built-in bullshit detector added an extra dimension to her ability to work her way through a problem.

Sheriff Brandt Morgan, one of Joelle's two husbands, had laughed one night when they'd been sitting at the club's bar watching the two women chatting across the room.

"Joelle walked away from Mensa because she thought it was boring; Tally would stay just to torment the members into livening things up. I've listened to the two of them discuss the medical ethics of pharmaceuticals and not understood a word they said. Honest to God, it sounded like English, but I was completely lost. It was damned humbling."

Brandt's reputation as a SEAL team leader was still spoken about with a tone bordering on reverence, and Koi knew the man was no intellectual slouch. Brandt and Koi had never worked together, but he understood what the other man was trying to say.

"Karl was intimidated by her. I know he respected her, and from what I could see, he loved her. But he always seemed to be trying to 'one-up' her, and over time, it took a toll." Koi remembered feeling in his gut that Brandt had just handed him the keys to understanding Tally Tyson—and he'd done it deliberately.

Brushing back the long, blonde tendrils of hair that drifted around the edges of her face, Koi smiled down at Tally as she worried her lip, trying to focus on the questions rearing up in her mind. As a kinesthetic learner, Tally problem solved best when she was moving. He'd seen her pace for hours as she worked through the details of how to best treat a particularly challenging patient.

"Come on, *ma poupée*." Grabbing her hand, he headed to the door. "Let's go for a walk, it'll help you think, and moonlight is good for the soul."

Chapter Ten

MIA LET TUCKER and Brock lead her from the room, grateful they weren't going to watch another scene. She would spontaneously combust if she had to watch another ménage. Sweet Mother Mary, she'd almost come watching Master Cam flog CeCe, and now, she was embarrassed to have been crushing on her new friend's man. She could try to blame the alcohol, but the truth was easier.

It wasn't Cameron Barnes who'd mesmerized her, it was the Master… the confident sexual Dominant who'd kept her totally enthralled during the scene. The catlike grace of his movements, the set of his shoulders contrasting against his complete focus on CeCe had riveted her. No wasted movements, every breath appeared to be choreographed for maximum efficiency and impact.

Dating had always been such an incredible disappointment for Mia, and now, she was beginning to suspect why. She'd never dated an alpha male because she'd only dated men her grandfather had previously approved. Her last date had interrupted their make out session to take a phone call… from his mother, for heaven's sake.

After that, Mia had decided to stick with the men in her romance novels and forgo the real ones who always seemed to let her down. Most of the men she dated were candid about their motives, wanting to get close to her grandfather for one reason or another. The only one who'd indicated any interest in sex for the sake of pleasure had wanted her to fuck him with a used strap-on he'd picked it up at a pawn shop. He'd pulled it from the trunk of his car to show her his bargain; she'd taken a taxi home. Years later, the memory still made her shudder with revulsion.

"I don't know what she's thinking about, but it's not how to best please her Masters. Did you see the look on her pretty face? Move her over closer to the railing, let's see what we can do about bringing our sub's sharp mind back into focus."

Brock's words were spoken loud enough for anyone nearby to hear, and the words made her pussy convulse as if he'd stroked his fingers along the sensitive walls. A warm rush of cream coated the newly denuded lips of her labia, and Mia once again thanked the stars above she was barefoot, or she might have stumbled right over the edge into the dark rolling water.

Mia looked out over the slow cresting of the waves and felt her breath catch. "It's so beautiful. The light dancing over the surface makes me wonder if the forest fairies have come out to play on the water."

Brock smiled down at her. "Our mom always told us God scattered diamonds on the water at night to lead sailors home. I think that was one of the reasons we wanted to be SEALs."

Mia's heart melted at the sentiment. Surely any man who spoke so sweetly about his mother wouldn't embarrass her too badly out here in the open, right? The thought had no sooner floated through her mind than the two of them stopped abruptly. Shifting, so they were standing shoulder to shoulder with their backs to the open area where other couples were milling about, both men crossed bulging arms over their chests as they studied her.

"We've reviewed the contents of your e-reader," Tucker broke the silence first, "so we know you are familiar with at least the basics of the lifestyle, sweet cheeks. We'll be using the stoplight system for safe words. Tell me what you understand that to mean."

Mia wasn't sure if it was his commanding tone or her soul-deep need to please, but she didn't hesitate to explain what she'd read time and again in the erotic novels.

"If I become overwhelmed either physically or emotionally, I should say 'red,' and that brings everything to an immediate halt. And if I'm approaching my limit, I can say 'yellow' to let you know I'm getting close to safewording out."

Brock nodded, and she saw a shift in his posture that told her their charade was about to become much more real. His voice was quieter than it had been a few minutes earlier… when it had been obvious he'd intended for those around them to hear what he was saying.

"Do you understand the difference between an erotic spanking and a punishment spanking?" He must have seen the flair of uncertainty in her eyes because before she could take a step back, his one-word, clipped command locked her feet in place. "Don't."

"Answer the question, Mia. Stop thinking and just respond," Tucker's words were spoken softly, but their steel core was impossible to miss.

"I understand the concept, but I'm not sure I believe there is a difference."

Brock's nostrils flared, and the feral grin that spread over Tucker's face probably should have worried her. She'd read so many stories where the Dom claimed to be rewarding his or her submissive with a spanking, Mia had almost decided the word was code for something else.

How could anyone consider being smacked on the ass a reward? It didn't make any sense if you asked her. But then, CeCe looked like she'd certainly enjoyed the flogging, so maybe there was something to the whole erotic pain concept.

But how much is too much? The whole thing sounds awfully intimate for role-playing, and I'm not very good at hiding my emotions, so maybe I'd better skip anything that's going to muddle up my mind. These guys are being paid to deliver me to their bosses in Texas, then they'll be done. I'll feel like I did something wrong, and they'll feel like they have to avoid the clinging Colombian vine. Holy shit, can this get any more convoluted? How do I know what I'm supposed to do? I've never been any good at this, and now, my life and the life of a man I've only met once for a few short minutes may depend on me pulling off this ruse.

"And this nonsense is why you need a good paddling," Brock's stern voice brought her out of her musings. "Where on Earth did you go?" When she blinked at him in surprise, Tucker used his fingers under her chin to direct her attention in his direction.

"Contrary to most people expect, my brother has the heavier hand, so you're going over my lap instead of his. I'm not going to give you a number, you'll have to trust me to know when you've had enough."

Enough? Oh dear, this sounds ominous.

"No, sweet cheeks. You'll recognize ominous when you see it."

Just fucking dandy, now my subconscious is talking out loud.

TUCKER SCOOTED THE nearest deck chair aside since the thing was six inches off the ground. Hell, even as petite as Mia was, her chin would probably scrape on the ground if he pulled her over his lap that close to the wood plank surface. There was a bench a few feet from a glass-paneled railing; she'd be able to look over the water, adding another dimension to the experience. Even in the dim light, he could see her mind was already spinning off in another direction, so he didn't waste any time on preliminaries. Pulling her over his lap, Tucker scooted her forward until her ass was peaked perfectly for the fall of his hand. He smiled at her squeak of surprise.

"Hold still, Kodak. I'm going to see what I can do about your little focus problem." Her dress had already risen far enough to bare the bottom half of her ass cheeks, and he used the calloused pads of his fingers to push the light fabric up to her lower back. Slowing the movement gave her mind time to process his touch as a caress rather than letting her stumble over her embarrassment at being exposed.

Tucker loved the way her skin looked in the moonlight, the way the soft glow highlighted her beautiful curves. Fuck, he'd keep her naked and bathed in pearlescent light if he could—she was absolutely glowing. He trailed his fingers through her slick folds and chuckled.

"I think our little sub likes having her bare ass upended to the breeze. She's soaking wet, and I'm looking forward to feeling all that slippery sweetness coat my fingers when she comes."

Out of the corner of his eye, he saw Brock rearrange himself, and Tuck understood his brother's dilemma since his own cock was straining the confines of the pants Cam had given him. Without giving her a chance to worry about what was to come, Tucker landed a swat on the fleshiest part of her perk ass.

She jerked in his hold and gasped, but he knew her reaction was more from surprise than pain. The swat he'd given her had been solid, but it hadn't been harsh.

"Stay still, sweet cheeks." He rested his palm over the heat from the first swat for several seconds, giving her body a chance to register the warmth spreading to her nearby pussy. Another swat, this one more stinging than the first, made her gasp, and he admonished her, "Don't clench your muscles, Mia. Let go of your fear and breathe."

"Easy for you to say. Your pink bits aren't waving in the wind for everyone parading by to see, and somebody twice your size isn't using his baseball sized mitt to paddle you." Her indignant response earned her three sharp swats, delivered in quick succession. She'd certainly notice the difference between these and the two she'd gotten before.

"We'll always take your sass out on your lovely ass, baby. You're lucky it's Tucker's lap your draped over and not mine. I take a dim view of cheeky answers," Brock's tone was strained, and Tucker would tease him later that it was a result of oxygen deprivation to the brain since all his blood was likely pooled a lot farther south.

"Yes, Sir."

Tucker hated the sniffle he heard in her response. Dammit, this wasn't supposed to be about pain, but there had been witnesses to her flippant answer, so they hadn't dared let it go.

"Behave, sweet cheeks." Leaning down, he lightly bit the shell of her ear. "When you speak out in front of the other guests, we'll have no choice but to meet the challenge. We don't want to punish you, pet. We'd much rather make your body sing with pleasure. I'm looking forward to feeling you come around my fingers and hearing your soft cries as the pleasure rolls over you in wave after wave of ecstasy."

When she shuddered, he set a steady pace of strikes, making sure his palm never landed in the same place twice in a row. By the seventh swat, he could smell the musky scent of her heat. Glistening trails of her cream were silver rivulets coating the insides of her thighs and dampening his knee.

"She's soaking wet. Fuck, I can see it from here," Brock's voice was filled with desire, and Tucker knew it was testing his brother's patience to stand to the side. Brock's palm fell harder than Tucker's, and as a newbie, Mia needed a lighter touch for this introduction. Slipping his fingers through her slick folds, Tucker groaned when she squirmed against his cock. Jesus, Joseph, and Mary, those wiggles were going to make him come before he could get inside her, and he hadn't done that since he was sixteen.

Pushing his fingers inside her rippling vagina, Tucker zeroed in on his spongy target. Pressing against her G-spot, he snapped, "Come for me, pet." He'd barely gotten the words out when Mia's entire body answered his command. Her cry of release was the sweetest sound he'd ever heard, and Tucker suddenly regretted not being able to see her face. Next time he made her come, Tuck wanted her eyes locked on his.

When she sagged over his knee, Tucker leaned back and let Brock roll her into his arms. Instead of sitting down to give Mia the aftercare she deserved, his brother stalked toward the sliding doors on the starboard side of the deck. Brock was halfway down the hall by the time Tucker caught up.

"Damn, where's the fire?" Tucker hoped his brother would regain some measure of control before they entered the suite, or he was going to burst into flames, and Mia would be caught in the firestorm.

For the past year, Brock had been the one with the cool head, and as a result, he'd taken the lead when they'd played at the club. Tucker hadn't cared about anything remotely emotional, wanting nothing but the brief escape sex provided. As soon as it was over, Tucker excused himself, happily leaving the cuddling to Brock. But everything about Mia felt different and even as reluctant as Tucker was to admit it, she drew him like a magnet to steel.

Clasping his hand on his brother's shoulder when he stopped in front of the door to their suite, Tucker gave Brock a look he hoped screamed *rein it in*. Some of the lust-crazed look in Brock's eyes cleared, and the curt nod of his brother's head was probably the only assurance Tuck would get.

"Open the door, or I'm going to fuck her in the hall," Brock's growled words elicited an immediate response from Mia, but it was the polar opposite from what Tucker expected. The little sub, whose ass had to still be smarting from the spanking he'd given her, giggled. *Giggled!*

MIA FELT LIKE she'd been run over by a dump truck filled with boulders after the most spectacular orgasm of her life. She'd sagged over Tucker's lap, trying to pull the fragmented pieces of her mind back together when she suddenly realized Brock was picking her up. Nobody's brain could function after being blown into tiny bits and scattered over the dark water of the Caribbean Sea, and she hadn't had enough energy to protest.

When Brock stopped in front of what she assumed was the door to their suite, the tension was vibrating from him in waves. She started to worry he was angry she'd come like a common streetwalker until she heard him admonish his brother to open the door before he fucked her in the hall. Relief swept over her, knowing he wasn't angry, and thanks to the chaos her hormones were causing, she giggled rather than keeping her gratitude in check.

Brock's lips pressed against her forehead before he shook his head and smiled down at her.

"There is a time for giggling, baby, and this is *not* it. I'm skating on a very fine edge. Watching Tuck bring you to a screaming climax shredded my control. Unless you want me to pin you to the wall and fuck you until neither one of us can walk, you'll keep quiet until my slower-than-molasses-in-winter brother opens the damned door."

Mia didn't know anything about molasses in winter, but she kept her question to herself as Tucker muttered an oath, then shouldered past Brock to scan his card in the lock.

Mia's first view of the suite took her breath away. They'd planned to stop here before eating, but her growling stomach had protested, and they'd headed directly to the restaurant. The spacious suite's marble floors gleamed in the soft light from the wall sconces, and her eyes immediately went to the glass accordion doors opened to showcase an enormous balcony overlooking the water. Brock must have followed her gaze because he snorted a laugh as he set her on her feet.

"Next time, sweetheart. Strip."

Next time? What did that mean? Her mind finally

caught up, and she realized he must have thought she wanted to have sex on the deck. Which she did. But that wasn't what she'd been thinking. She'd simply been admiring the view. The sound of tearing fabric reached her ears a split second before she heard Brock growl, "Too slow, baby." The dress she'd been wearing fell around her feet in tatters, and she blinked up at him in utter disbelief.

Tucker burst out laughing, and Brock muttered something she hadn't been able to hear, but it didn't stem his brother's laughter.

"You're supposed to be the romantic one, asshole. Hell, who knew you'd get so worked up watching a moonlight spanking. Give her a minute to get her bearings before ordering her to strip in the middle of an unfamiliar room, you Neanderthal." He glanced her way, his heated gaze raking over her from the tips of her French manicured toes to the top of her head. The slow perusal made Mia's blood run hot, and she knew she'd flushed at the close scrutiny. "Although I must admit, naked looks beautiful on her. Turn around, pet. I want to check your ass for marks."

She gasped and tried to take a step back, but what sounded like a growl kept her rooted in place.

"He wants to make sure there won't be any bruising from your erotic spanking, baby. Turn around, so we can see if we need to treat you with arnica cream." She knew the healing powers of arnica, but the thought of these two big men rubbing cream into her tender tissues made her knees wobble when she tried to turn. Brock's warm hand cupped her elbow, steadying her as she shuffled her bare feet over the cool marble.

Mia heard Tucker move closer and felt the soft brush of cool air over her heated posterior as he knelt behind her. *Holy shit, could this get any more embarrassing?* His fingers trailed over her skin, and she flinched when they moved over a particularly painful spot.

"She's going to be sore tomorrow, but the tenderness will remind her of how beautifully her body blurred the line between pain and pleasure." The rustle of clothing was her only indication he was once again standing until he pressed a kiss to her shoulder.

"You were absolutely amazing. You are meant for this lifestyle, sweet cheeks." She noted he hadn't said she was meant to be theirs, and something about that tore a hole in her heart, but she pushed those thoughts aside. Mia was determined to enjoy the cruise and squeeze every bit of pleasure she could from the experience because the chance of her getting another opportunity like this one was slim to none. Was she going to milk all the enjoyment she could from this chance? *Damned Skippy.*

Chapter Eleven

Lucia Mendez glared at the man who'd been his chief of security for years. Joseph Moreno might be a retired general, but he was also an arrogant bastard of the first order. Moreno's penchant for younger women had never set well with Lucia's sweet wife, and she'd warned him—too many times to count—the man he considered a trusted friend was a wolf in sheep's clothing. Joseph had worked for Lucia for years, but lately, the man often forgot which one of them was in charge.

"Do not tell me you don't know, Joseph. I am not interested in your excuses. Find out why the incompetent men you hired allowed Mia to board a cruise ship that set sail moments later." A ship leased to a man everyone mistakenly believed had retired from the CIA. Anyone with any international experience at all knew Cameron Barnes was as much an agent now as he'd ever been although he seemed to keep a much lower profile.

"The men escorting her were obviously well-trained. She slipped through our fingers at her apartment by hiding under the floor. The men I'd sent to bring her in for her own safety underestimated your lovely granddaughter. They will not make the same mistake again."

Moreno tried but seemed unable to completely blank his expression. Lucia would start making calls as soon as the man left for the night. Mia had tried to tell him something about the man sitting on the other side of the desk, but he'd been too busy to listen. She might be on the run, but she was still under his watchful eye.

Pressing his palm against his chest, Lucia cursed the spicy dinner he hadn't been able to resist. His cook kept trying to feed him bland dishes at night, but Lucia was not yet ready to admit his body was no longer that of a young man. Joseph Moreno's eyes followed the circular movements with avid interest, and for the first time since he'd met Joseph, Lucia felt a chill of fear in his presence. It was time to replace Morena, but Lucia needed to make a phone call first, and tipping Joseph off wouldn't be wise.

"You are dismissed, my friend. Go to town and enjoy the ladies who follow you like a gaggle of geese." The arrogant sloth smiled at the compliment and slowly got to his feet. He'd be out of the compound within minutes without a backward glance, giving Lucia the opening he needed to call Cam. It was time for the man whose life he'd once saved to answer a few questions.

WITH A LITTLE luck, maybe the old bastard would die before Joseph got his hands on Mia. His boss's granddaughter was proving herself far more resourceful than Joseph had anticipated. Helping rescue Senator Tyson had put her on the radar of several organizations she should have steered clear of, but like all journalists, she hadn't been able to keep her nose out of places it didn't belong. Christ, it was bad enough she'd almost walked in on his own operation; it had been pure luck he'd seen her reflection in a shop window late one-night walking down the street. He'd been shocked to discover she'd managed to follow him without being detected and grateful he'd seen her in time to change course.

Joseph knew he'd been stalling when it came to a decision about how to deal with Mia, hoping she would find some other shiny object to chase, and now she'd slipped through his fingers. The only way he could think of to reel her in was to make certain her grandfather needed her, and the drug he'd slipped into the old man's after dinner brandy should do just that. Everything in Lucia Mendez's life was mind-numbingly predictable. Ordinarily, Joseph found Lucia's routine appallingly drab, but tonight it would play in his favor. The old man would sit by the fire sipping his drink and before the night was over, he'd be clinging to life by a thread. *Perfect.*

CAM LEANED BACK in his chair and let his gaze move over the woman sleeping on the nearby sofa. She was curled into the corner, looking more like a teenager than one of the most skilled and well-respected pediatric surgeons in the world. She was God's gift to sick and injured children, and Cam had always known he couldn't steal her away from those deserving souls. He was even more grateful she was an unearned gift to him. Cam might not have done anything to deserve Cecelia's love, but he wasn't ever going to question the cosmic decision to send her his way.

An hour ago, he'd answered the call he'd been expecting since Mia Mendez boarded the ship he'd chartered. He'd known her grandfather for years, and more importantly, he respected Lucia for fighting back against the cartels who often steamrolled good people. Lucia was one of the few international bankers who hadn't fallen prey to the greed so prevalent in the world's largest banks.

Lucia Mendez had held out against those who would have made the self-made man little more than a puppet at the expense of his own country. But resisting criminal forces had also made him a target, and Cam's concern for the other man had prompted the second call of the evening. Kent and Kyle West already had two men watching the Mendez estate and sent them to check on the elderly man before they'd finished speaking with Cam. Lucia's repeated comments about his heartburn had been red flags to Cam, and the Wests had readily agreed.

Turning to watch the crackling flames in the fireplace, Cam thought back on the first time he met Mia. He'd watched her descend the stairs during her quinceanera, and he still remembered the intelligence he'd seen swirling in her blue eyes. Cam had met the young woman several more times over the years in various disguises, and he'd been relieved she hadn't recognized him out on the dock. He'd used the shadows to his advantage, but he doubted her eye for detail would be fooled for long.

Letting his thoughts drift back to the woman sleeping peacefully nearby. Cam was becoming frustrated the inquiries he'd made into real estate in Houston weren't yielding anything interesting, and it looked as if they were going to have to build. When he'd casually mentioned it to Kent before they ended their call, his friend had told him to hold-up on a decision because he had an idea. *There's a terrifying thought.* Many assumed Kent wasn't as sharp or as ruthless in business as his brother simply because his involvement wasn't as overt. The two were mirror images in almost every way. Physically, they were nearly impossible to tell apart, contrary to what their firestorm of a wife would tell you.

Kent and Kyle's minds also worked at the same warp

speed. It was their method of attack when dealing with a problem that differed. Kyle was all about the blitz and frontal. Kent was much subtler, and in Cam's opinion, that made him much more dangerous. Both men were loyal friends and formidable enemies, and if Kent said he had an idea, Cam would wait to hear him out.

When his phone vibrated beside him, Cam picked it up and frowned at the message displayed on the screen.

Subject being transported to ER. Drink secured for testing. Last known visitor COS. Will update ASAP.

If everyone and their dog wasn't looking for her, Cam would be tempted to return to Colombia, so Mia could look after her grandfather, but that wasn't an option. He had put feelers out, trying to find out more about Lucia's Chief of Security. Cam had disliked the man on sight and told Lucia so, but Mendez hadn't taken the warning seriously. Hopefully, the elderly man wasn't going to pay for that mistake with his life.

Getting to his feet, Cam shook off the concerns. There was no reason to tell Mia about her grandfather until he knew more, and he wasn't looking forward to explaining how he'd come upon the information. He had hoped to deliver her safely to the Wests before laying his cards on the table, but it seemed fate had other plans. Leaning over CeCe, he pressed a kiss to her forehead as he lifted her into his arms.

"Come, pet. Time for bed." When her eyes fluttered open and her lips curved into a soft smile, he kissed her again. "Thank you for keeping me company, love."

"How is Mia's grandfather?" *Fuck. My, did I believe she would sleep through something this important?*

Chapter Twelve

MIA WAS DIZZY with desire; she'd been worried the men wouldn't show any interest in her when they were alone, but that diminished the moment they stepped across the threshold into the suite. One of the first things she'd learned as a photographer was how easily people could lie with their words and actions, but their eyes always revealed the truth.

Looking in Brock and Tucker's eyes told her their attraction to her had nothing to do with the fact she needed their protection or her grandfather's wealth. For the first time she could remember, she knew she was facing men who understood what she needed.

"She's thinking again," Tucker's voice startled her, and she jumped but caught herself before she would have taken a step back. "Good girl. Don't ever step away from your Dom, and unless we tell you otherwise, we want your eyes on ours. We need to be able to see when you drift away from us," his tone held just a hint of teasing, and she felt herself relax.

"I don't know what it is about you that turns my brother into fucking Dr. Phil," Brock shook his head and let out a disgusted sound as he wrapped his hand around her wrist and tugged her against his chest, "but I don't think I've ever heard him so chatty about protocol. I'm tired of all this talking. The two of you put on one hell of a show on deck, and I'm past ready to get my hands on you. Let's go." The next thing she knew, he was practically race-walking down the short hall and into a surprisingly spacious bedroom.

Taking in her surroundings, Mia noted the bank of windows and wondered what the view would be like in the morning. Looking out over the water would be a great way to wake up unless the sun was shining in her eyes. *I hate it when that happens.* A whoosh of air was her only warning before the burn of Brock's palm scorched her left ass cheek.

"I swear to all things holy, I'm going to light your pretty pink ass on fire if you don't stay with us, baby."

"Sorry. I was just wondering about the windows. And the view. And whether or not the sun would shine in my eyes in the morning because that's really annoying." Another swat proceeded Tucker's roar of laughter.

"Kodak, I don't think I've ever seen my brother turn that particular shade of purple. Even if you weren't the hottest woman I've ever had the pleasure of paddling, this would be worth the price of admission." Without saying another word, Tucker pulled her out of his brother's embrace and into his own.

"Pay attention, big brother. You want to keep the lady engaged, this is how it's done." His lips met hers, and Mia swore she heard music playing as he teased the seam with his tongue and pushed forward when she gasped. She'd been kissed before, but this was seduction and conquering, all in one sweet package. When he growled against her, the vibration in his chest made her nipples tingle, and she felt them tighten into stiff peaks.

The kiss was raging out-of-control, and Mia could have sworn she was falling. When her back came up against the cool cotton sheets covering the bed, she realized the sensation hadn't been her overactive imagination. How had he managed to move her across the room without her knowing? Damn, that was humbling, but at this moment, she was past the point of caring about anything vaguely resembling self-awareness or improprieties. When she finally opened her eyes, she blinked back her surprise; it wasn't Tucker's face, but Brock's looking down on her.

"Damn, I do love that look," he smiled. "So utterly lost in the moment, she's not tracking our movements. *Perfect.*" His lips sealed over hers, and Brock's kiss was just as powerful as his brother's. Tucker had pushed, but Brock cajoled. Despite his earlier desperation, he was all cool control and tantalizing temptation now.

Tucker reminded her of the bad boy girls loved, but she suspected it was Brock who dried their tears when Tucker moved on. Brock was the one who would hold her when she was sad and be the first to celebrate her successes. Realizing she was letting her head get way ahead of things, Mia refocused herself on enjoying the moment.

Reaching up, she cupped his shoulders and smiled into the kiss when she realized he'd taken off his shirt. She tried to slide her arms around him and was surprised when her wrists were shackled by large hands and pulled over her head. Rather than frightening her, she felt a burst of heat sear her nerve endings, and she arched into Brock's kiss. Soul shattering need took over and erased anything vaguely resembling logic from her mind.

The rustling of clothing and the crinkling of a condom wrapper pulled her out of the haze of arousal, making her realize Brock had ended the kiss.

"Damn, baby, you make a man lose his mind for wanting you."

When she finally let her gaze stray from his rich chocolate eyes, she was surprised to see his enormous cock was already sheathed in a condom, the wide tip poised at her entrance. He must have sensed her alarm because he chuckled.

"It'll fit, baby, I promise."

She wasn't a virgin, but she was far from experienced. The only other time she'd had sex, it hadn't been anything she was interested in repeating, so she hadn't bothered. It helped that she hadn't met anyone interesting enough to make her reconsider her self-imposed celibacy... until Brock and Tucker. When she decided to end a dry spell, she did it in grand style, with not one smokin' hot man, but two.

"Eyes on me, sweetheart. I need to know this is what you want, Mia. I'm sensing your hesitance, and even though I'm about to burst, wanting to sink into your heat, I'm not moving until you say the words."

Aww. Mia recognized this because she'd grown up having to repeat the *magic words* to get things done. "Please." The word was little more than a whisper and sounded like a plea even to her own ears.

"As lovely as that sounded, and I assure you, hearing you ask so sweetly is damned tempting, I need more." Brock's brows drew together, and she could tell he was struggling to maintain control.

The harder she tried to figure out what he wanted, the faster her mind spun out of control. At this rate, she'd burst into flames from the heat of the tip of his cock slipping slowly against her folds. Her hips canted of their own volition, and he shook his head.

"Tell me that you want this, Mia. Say the words. I'm not going to fuck you until you ask."

Ask him to fuck her? Could she speak so crudely to get what she wanted? She'd promised herself she wasn't going to skimp on the pleasure these men could offer, and it wasn't a secret that was going to involve wild monkey sex. So why was she balking about saying the one word needed to set things in motion?

"There she goes overthinking things again. Damn, I see a lot of spankings in her future," Tucker's amused tone grated on her last nerve. Her body was shuddering with unmet need and he was yammering about spankings?

"Chicken noodle soup, please fuck me before I die," the words tumbled out without hitting the filter she usually kept firmly in place between her mouth and her brain, but Tucker's taunt had short-circuited her ability to edit her words. In the end, it didn't matter because any excuse she might have eventually voiced evaporated into a fine mist when Brock pushed himself past her entrance. The burn of stretching tissues made her breath catch, and even lost in the chaos of her body's reactions, Mia felt both men go completely still.

"As amusing as that answer was, I'm not moving until you convince me you're okay."

Mia struggled to smile through the haze. It wasn't that she was in pain, it was just taking her a few minutes to adjust to his size. The sweet burn of her tightly stretched tissues felt exquisite.

"So big. So good. Oh God, please don't stop." She lost sight of Brock's face and realized her eyes had rolled back so far, it was no wonder the world had gone dark around her.

"We're going to go slow no matter how many times you tempt me, baby. You are so fucking tight," Brock's voice was harsh, but she knew it wasn't from anger. Her heart appreciated his care even if her body wasn't as appreciative of the delay.

"When is the last time you had sex, sweet cheeks?" Tucker's words were spoken against the sensitive spot behind her ear and sent a spear of longing straight to her nipples. What was with these two? None of the books she'd read had prepared her for all this chit-chat. *What the hell? I thought American men were supposed to be about less talk and more action? Isn't there a song about that? Don't these guys listen to the radio?*

Tucker's rumbling laughter made her groan.

"Please tell me I didn't say that out loud? Dumplings, I have to start paying more... oh God, please don't stop." Brock was pulling back, and she struggled to free her hands, so she could clamp them over him and hold him in place.

"How long, sweet cheeks?"

"College. Freshman year." She hoped their background on her didn't include her educational history because if it did...

"You were barely seventeen years old when you started college, for fuck's sake. What ass wipe had sex with a girl that age?" Tucker sounded outraged and his words were tantamount to someone throwing a bucket of cold water over her.

The adrenaline from the arousal she'd felt a few seconds before, fell away and a waterfall of tears followed. She hated to cry. *Hated it.* It infuriated her that she was displaying such weakness after all she'd been through over the past few weeks. She tried to turn her face away from Tucker, but Brock's warm hands bracketed her face and held her still.

"Look at me, baby." When she tried to shake her head,

and wiggle out from under him, his voice deepened. "Right now, Mia. Open your eyes and let my hot-headed brother apologize." She pulled in a shuddering breath and slowly lifted her tear-soaked lashes. Brock's eyes were filled with indulgence. "Our protective instincts are going to override our good sense sometimes, baby."

Tucker turned her face, so he could look into her eyes. "Christ, sweet cheeks, I'm sorry. I just hated feeling like some prick had taken advantage of you. I know you are a capable woman, and it's not any of my business what happened, but damnit, I still want to rip his head off." This time his repentant smile took the sting out of the words. She hadn't been taken advantage of by an older man, she and the boy who'd reluctantly claimed her virginity were the same age.

"It wasn't his fault, but I don't want to talk about this with you... either of you. If you'll just let me go, I'm tired, and I'd like to get some sleep. I'm sure Mr. Barnes will have a lot of questions for me tomorrow, and I'd like to be able to think clearly during what is sure to be an intense interrogation."

As apologies went, Tucker Deitz's sucked. Mia's anger wasn't ebbing, and if they didn't leave her alone pretty damned fast, she was going to start crying again, then she'd be even more pissed off. She rarely cried when she was sad, but since she'd been raised to hold back her anger, tears were the only outlet for the emotion. It was a never-ending cycle until she'd cried herself into a coma and slept it off.

TUCKER FELT LIKE a first-class ass. He'd reacted with a flash of fiery possessiveness he hadn't even felt for the woman he'd married. The harsh words had slipped out before his brain could kick into gear and hold them back. Seeing Mia's tears of frustration and the hurt reflected in her eyes made him want to put his fist through a wall, and from the look on Brock's face, he'd better be ready to have his ass handed to him on that front as well.

If he was half the man he should be, he'd walk out the door and let Brock make love to Mia. He knew his brother, and there was no question his game plan had just taken a one-eighty. There wouldn't be any wild abandon fucking tonight—it had been too long since she'd taken a cock inside her sweet pussy, and it was doubtful her experience had been about pleasure. It said a lot about how selfish he could be to admit he wasn't going anywhere. Tucker was determined to make it up to her, he just wasn't sure how.

Chapter Thirteen

Brock was going to kick his brother's ass. He understood Tucker's reaction. Hell, in some ways he was grateful to see the intense emotional response from the man who'd all but tuned out since his broom-riding ex turned his world on end. And Brock knew he shared some responsibility for this massive fuck-up because it had been his question about her previous experience that set them on the road to nowhere. Now, it was a matter of damage control and beginning to repair the shredded trust they'd been building since pulling Mia out of that damned hole under her bedroom floor.

Listening to Tucker's lame apology tested his restraint because he could feel the frustration pulsing around Mia. She wasn't buying it, and Brock didn't blame her. When she politely dismissed them, he knew it was time to intervene. Smiling to himself, he wondered if this wasn't a sign of things to come. How often would he play peacemaker between the two of them? Of course, Tucker had mediated between them earlier during her erotic spanking, so perhaps it would all even out in the end. He'd never wanted a woman who was so blindly compliant, she never challenged him, and he knew Tucker wouldn't be attracted to a woman like that either.

"We're not going to let you hide, baby. I know Tuck's apology wasn't much, but I think he was as surprised by his outburst as you were. He hasn't been interested in caring for a woman for a while, but that's his story to tell, and I'm going to let him share it with you when he's ready. For now, let's just say he wasn't expecting to be so alarmed about your safety, even it was a long time ago."

He felt her begin to relax against him and he took advantage of the moment by sealing his lips over hers. The kiss started out as a peace offering but transitioned to an inferno of seduction in five seconds flat.

"Jesus, that's so fucking hot. I love watching you catch fire in my brother's arms, sweet cheeks. And I promise, I'll be a lot better at apologizing with my body than I am with words." Brock listened to Tucker's words and agreed his brother was better with action than words. No doubt his physical apology would be much more persuasive.

Brock didn't break the kiss but gave Mia a chance to pull in a quick breath before pulling her right back into the web he was weaving around them. The short cruise to Texas wasn't going to give them a tremendous amount of time to explore the possibilities of a relationship with Mia, and Brock was determined to make the most of every minute. The first step was slipping down her slender body and making sure she was ready for him. Feeling her tongue dueling with his and feeling the vibration of her mews of desire pressing the tight peaks of her nipples against his chest made his cock so hard, the damned thing was throbbing against her thigh.

Kissing down the side of her neck and continuing down until he could trace the line of her collarbone with his tongue, he was pleased to hear Tucker shedding his clothes at the side of the bed. When the bed dipped, signaling Tuck's return, Brock moved further down, making room for Tucker to sample the sweet lips he'd been reluctant to leave.

"I'm going to kiss you, sweet cheeks. I can see the effect you had on Brock, and I'm looking forward to tasting these beautiful lips." By the time Brock's tongue was circling Mia's navel, Tucker was whispering sweet words to her, and the scent of her arousal was once again filling the air. Trailing the tip of his tongue through her wet folds, Brock felt her shudder and heard Tucker's chuckle.

"He's just getting started darlin.' Just wait until he fucks you with his tongue, you're going to have an out-of-body experience, it's going to feel so good." Brock gave Tuck a quick hand signal then pushed his tongue deep into her tight channel.

"Come for us, Mia." Tucker's simple command was all it took for Mia to shatter in their arms. Her pussy sent a flood of sweet cream over his tongue, and Brock relished her unique flavor. With his hands wrapped around her slender thighs, he could feel the fine tremors in her muscles as she slowly floated back to herself.

He wanted her cognizant but still riding the wave when he pushed deep inside her. It had been so long since she'd been with a man, and even though he was a bit narrower than his brother, he was still larger than average, so he was going to have to go slow, giving her rapidly swelling tissues time to stretch enough to accommodate him.

Moving back into position, Brock positioned himself at her opening and started the slow process of rocking his hips forward and back, claiming another fraction of an inch each time he pressed further in. When he felt her beginning to tense, he slowed and nodded to Tucker.

"I think our little sub needs something to distract her, brother." The walls of her vagina contracted around him so tight, it was almost painful, and a groan of pleasure slipped out before he could call it back.

"She is tightening around me like a damned vice, and I'm not even halfway inside. This is going to be over much too soon if you don't give her something else to think about."

"Here, sweet cheeks, give me a little taste of the heaven I see in your other Master's eyes and suck me." Brock would have cheered Tucker's subtle reference to himself as her Master if he hadn't been so focused on not plunging in as deep as he could go and fucking her like the beast simmering below the surface. If he didn't move soon, his damned head was going to explode.

TUCKER'S EYES ROLLED up when the tip of Mia's tongue teased his tip, lapping at the pearly drop, and humming appreciation. Holding himself close to her lips with one hand while keeping her arms above her head with the other meant he was able to control how much she could torment him with the wicked flicks of her tongue along the corona. Feeling the heat of her mouth so close as she'd traced her tongue along the rigid ring surrounding the head of his penis was driving him slowly out of his mind.

Painting a second drop of pre-cum over her lips and seeing it glisten in the dim light was one of the most erotic things he'd ever experienced. Watching his brother slowly push his way inside her pussy and listening to the sexy sounds she made was pushing his control to the limit. Mia might not have a lot of sexual experience, but she had amazing instincts.

"Damn, sweet cheeks, your mouth is so hot, you're

burning me alive. Relax your jaw and breath through your nose, I want to see how far you can take me."

Normally her eyes were a bright blue, but arousal had darkened them until they were deep violet. She blinked up at him and gave a quick nod without releasing him, and he felt her relax around him.

Without giving her a chance to worry about what he was going to do, Tuck began pushing forward until he knew he was at the back of her throat.

"Swallow around me, pet. You are fucking amazing." When she swallowed, her throat muscles squeezed him, and Tucker's head fell back on his shoulders as he moaned her name. "Fuck me, Mia, that feels so good, I have no way to even begin to describe it." Pulling back, the vibration of her groaned protest sent most of his remaining blood to his cock, and he hoped like hell he wouldn't pass out.

"You are killing me, sweet cheeks. That mouth is pure pleasure." Sliding almost all the way out and then pushing back in, Tucker wanted to praise her for the way she opened her throat to welcome him, but any ability he'd had to form a coherent thought, let alone speak, had evaporated into a fine mist in the heat.

"I was hoping this would help me stave off my release but watching the way she is making love to you with her mouth is giving me almost as much pleasure as feeling her muscles rippling around me. Every time we speak to her, she answers with her whole body. Her vaginal muscles tremble, her thighs clench against me, and I see her fingers flexing in your hold. I swear to God if she could get her hands on us, we'd both snap."

His words must have been enough to set her off because before he'd finished speaking, he felt the first wave of her release. Brock had finally pushed himself in so that his tip was pressing against her cervix and as soon as she started to go over, he set a steady pace that would extend her orgasm without damaging the tightly stretched tissues.

Looking up at her face, he saw her cheeks hollow, and Tucker's head once again fell back on his shoulders.

"Sweet cheeks, if you don't want to swallow, you'd better let go." A split second later Tucker swore a blue streak worthy of the sailor he'd once been. Before Brock would comment, his brother shouted his release, and Mia's body stiffened beneath his, triggering his own trip into sweet oblivion.

Brock couldn't remember the last time he'd been blindsided by a release. He was known for being able to hold back until the woman he was with had come at least three times, but watching Mia pleasure his brother had tipped him over without warning. The last fragments of his mind were all that kept him from rutting her like an animal. When he'd finally spent himself into the condom, he collapsed onto her, barely catching himself on his forearms so she wasn't flattened by his weight.

"I think I flew through heaven, but I'm not sure I'll live to tell about it. Holy fucking hell, baby," Brock's voice was surprisingly coherent considering every single one of his brain cells was refusing to function.

Tucker stretched out beside her and lay staring blankly at the ceiling.

"If that's inexperience, she's going to kill us when she figures it all out. Not that I'm complaining. Hell, I'm looking forward to death by pleasure."

When he thought his legs would hold him, Brock slowly slid from her pussy and smiled at the aftershocks quaking through her sex.

"Don't tempt the beast, baby." Leaning down, he gave

her a quick kiss before stepping into the en-suite bathroom to dispose of the condom and wet a warm cloth. She made token protests when he cleaned and dried the tender tissues, but Tucker's warning growl kept her from moving.

Her eyes fluttered open when he returned to the bed, and the sweet smile curving her lips made his heart squeeze in his chest.

"That was remarkable. Can we do it again?" Brock blinked at her in surprise and laughed.

"Damn straight, baby. But let's let your body rest a bit so you'll be a better judge of what might be too much."

"That's right, Kodak. If we made love to you now, all those lovely endorphins floating around in your blood might inhibit your ability to recognize pain."

"I thought that was a good thing? All the books I've read talk about how pain and pleasure are two sides of the same coin." Mia's ability to think, when his own brain was numb, was damned impressive. Brock would have said as much if he'd been able to think clearly enough. Damn, the woman had fried his brain.

"You're right, but Brock stretched all those unused tissues, and right now, it would hard for you to distinguish between the sweet pain that leads to pleasure and pain that's supposed to serve as a warning to avoid injury." Tucker's explanation was dead-on, but Brock could only nod in agreement as he pressed himself against her back. She'd rolled against Tucker, using his shoulder as a pillow, and Brock loved the feeling of her sandwiched between them.

Looking over her, Brock watched Tucker gently push back the dark strands of her hair that had fallen over the face. The tender look in his brother's green eyes filled Brock with hope. Maybe the ice was finally cracking around his heart.

Chapter Fourteen

Sam McCall stood outside the doors of the Intensive Care Unit of the sprawling medical center in the middle of Medellin, Colombia, watching the firestorm he was married to charm her way into Lucia Mendez's personal physician's heart. The man had been steadfast in his refusal to tell Sam anything about Mendez's condition, so Sam brought in the team's secret weapon, Jen.

Jen worked for the State Department before joining the Prairie Winds team, and after being posted in South America, she easily assimilated into the varying cultures. Of course, the fact the prick she was conning was focused on her tits instead of her words wasn't helping the doctor maintain his resistance either. Sam and his younger brother Sage were both married to Jen, and at this moment, Mendez's personal physician owed his life to the fact it was Sam and not Sage standing back, watching him drool over what belonged to them.

When Sam saw Jen pat the other man's forearm, he knew she'd gotten the information she'd wanted and probably an invitation to dinner if she was true to form. Damn, the woman was fucking amazing even if she was sometimes a hazard to herself and others. There was a good reason the team had nicknamed her Miley—she was a wrecking ball in a gorgeous package.

She was grinning ear to ear when she stepped out of

the double doors, and he pulled her to the side and sealed his lips over hers before she had a chance to speak. By the time he let her go, she was shaking in his arms, and the other men in the waiting room were taunting them to *get a room*. When he finally let her go, he chuckled at the dazed look in her eyes.

"You kissed everything right out of my brain, husband mine. How's a girl supposed to act like a cool operator when you steal her mind?"

"I'm more interested in the hot woman hidden under the façade of a cool operator. And that doc was risking his life looking at you that way." When her cheeks turned pink, he chuckled. The woman had two husbands, and they enjoyed a very active ménage sex life, but she still blushed at his compliments. Damn, she was fucking perfect.

"Mendez was definitely poisoned, but it doesn't appear the attack was intended to kill him. Which makes me wonder if he wasn't being used as bait to lure his granddaughter home." Sam agreed and was already dialing his phone when she added, "The doctor mentioned Mr. Mendez woke up once, and the only word they could understand was Cam. They believe he was talking about a camera of some kind, but I'm guessing he was referring to Cameron Barnes." Sam raised a brow at her while he waited for the call to connect, and she rolled her eyes. "No, I didn't tell him. Geez, I'm not a dimwit, you know." He gave her a feral grin and held up one finger. He was keeping track, and that eye roll just cost her a trip over his knee.

Damn it's great to be me.

JOSEPH MORENO HUNG up the phone and cursed. According to the surveillance video, his boss had been taken to the hospital not long after Joseph had left the mansion, but that wasn't the problem. The fucking problem was the half hour of erased video from every camera around the sprawling estate. Their system was state-of-the-art, so it had taken someone with considerable skill and damned good equipment to hack into the feeds, erase only the portion that would have helped identify them, then back out without a trace. There weren't many people locally who could have accomplished it, and those who could have, wouldn't have bothered. And to top it all off, Lucia's personal physician was refusing to return his calls. Joseph wasn't being given any information about the man's status, and he was getting damned tired of getting the runaround.

Looking around Lucia's office, he noticed the old man's cell phone was missing, but could probably attribute that to one of the emergency medical personnel who'd responded to the anonymous call placed from a burner phone. If someone outside was helping the old man, the question was who? And why?

Suddenly remembering the drink he'd slipped the drug into, Joseph searched the room for the glass but didn't find it. Calling to the housekeeper, he inquired if she'd taken anything out of the office since arriving this morning, and she explained she hadn't cleaned the room yet. The calls he'd made to the ambulance service had ended in the same stonewalling he was getting from the hospital staff. He'd sent men to both locations with cash and for the first time in years, money had failed to yield answers.

Whoever was calling the shots was obviously throwing a lot of money into keeping Lucia's condition quiet. If it was the cartel, it was likely they had the same plan he had—to flush out Mia. But every feeler he'd put out was coming up empty—it defied logic. Something told him the man who'd delayed setting sail until Mia and her knights-in-fucking-shining-armor could board was involved in this, but the only thing Joseph knew about him was the name he'd used to charter the boat was an alias. Walking out of Lucia's office, Joseph felt the hair on the back of his neck stand on end, and he'd been a soldier long enough to heed the warning. It was time to find out who the players were, and the only way to do that was to get his hands on Mia Mendez.

Chapter Fifteen

MIA SAT BOLT upright in her chair and stared at the man sitting across from her as she tried to make sense of what he was saying. The same words kept replaying in her mind. *Grandfather. Hospital. Poisoned.*

"I have to go back."

"No," Brock and Tucker spoke at the same time from either side of her, and Cameron Barnes' smile annoyed her more than it should have. CeCe leaned against the desk beside her husband flipping through several pages of what looked like a medical report, but she hadn't so much as flinched at the outburst from the Deitz brothers.

"Yes. I'm his only living relative, and he needs me. I'm sorry if that doesn't fit your agenda, but I don't see that I have any choice. I'll catch a flight when we reach Cozumel tomorrow."

She could feel the frustration pulsing around her and briefly wondered if it was her own or if it was coming from the scowling men flanking her. CeCe continued to read, and her husband studied Mia as if she were some kind of mystery to be solved. There were a couple of other men she didn't recognize standing to the side of the small room, but it was Carl who broke the silence.

"Mia, let me play devil's advocate for a minute. Let's say I knew you had suddenly disappeared and my boss was breathing down my neck to bring you in. What would be the best way for me to lure you back out into the open?"

"Cane toads."

He blinked at her in surprise before a slow smile spread over his face.

"I bet your grandmother put her foot down on cursing, didn't she? Damn, that's great, and for the record, I know those little critters are nasty pieces of work." He gave her a minute to consider what he'd said, then pressed on, "You didn't answer my question, sweetie, and I suspect it isn't because you don't know the answer."

Oh, she knew the answer all right, but she was loath to admit he was right. *Dammit*.

"Hurting my grandfather would be the best way to get me to return to Colombia. But this seems like a lot of fuss just because I sent Senator Tyson's pictures to his wife."

She could understand the man's captors being pissed she'd helped him escape, but there wouldn't be anything to be gained by bringing her back. She'd already shared the best of the pictures. When she said as much, Cam cleared his throat to get her attention.

"Perhaps I can explain."

CeCe placed her small hand on her husband's forearm, causing him to shift his attention to her.

"Before you get into all the minutia of the soldier and spy games, let me put Mia's mind at ease about her grandfather. She'll be able to think with a clear head if she's not worrying about him."

"Pet, soldiers do not get into *minutia*." Mia almost laughed at the horrified look on Cameron's face. "Soldiers and operatives deal with facts and details. Not minutia."

Turning to Mia, CeCe smiled, and Mia almost laughed at the wicked gleam in her eyes as she carefully set the stack of papers aside.

"Whoever slipped him the drug wasn't trying to kill him. The toxicology report shows a low-level of a drug intended to imitate the symptoms of a heart attack without causing any real damage. I suspect he'd only ingested a small amount when he talked to Cam, who—being the brilliant man that he is—made your grandfather promise to not eat or drink anything else until help arrived."

"So, he's going to be okay?" For the first time since she'd walked into the room, Mia felt a tiny bit of tension drain away.

"Absolutely. Even worst-case scenario, your grandfather will be out of the hospital in a day or two, depending on how cautious his physician is." Mia knew her grandfather's doctor, and he might be an arrogant ass, but he wasn't a fool. The good doctor would be damned careful with the man who paid him an exorbitant amount of money for minimal health care.

"Thank you." Sagging with relief, Mia felt like a marionette whose strings had just been cut. "I can't tell you how relieved I am to know he'll be okay. We may not always see eye to eye, but I do love him to distraction." Returning her attention to Cam, Mia looked down and realized Brock and Tucker were each holding one of her hands. They'd lent her their strength even when she hadn't realized how much she needed it.

Turning her attention back to Cameron Barnes, Mia spoke, "You said you might be able to explain why someone would be anxious to lure me back to Colombia. Can you tell me what you meant?"

BROCK NOTED MIA hadn't referred to Colombia as home

and from the quick flair in Tucker's eyes, he knew his brother hadn't missed the small but significant slip as well. It made him wonder if she wasn't secretly relieved to be out from under her grandfather's thumb. Only time would tell.

Cam cleared his throat and let his eyes connect briefly with Brock's. At his quick nod, Cam began explaining what he'd briefed Brock and Tucker on early this morning while Mia was still sleeping.

"You mentioned you sent Tally the best shots you'd taken of her husband, and from what we found on your electronics, you did."

"You went through my camera and laptop? How did you access my computer files?" Brock wasn't sure if she was angry at the invasion of her privacy or curious about how they'd broken her password.

"Mia, I learned a long time ago people often miss important peripheral details because they are focused on their goal. You were looking for the best pictures of Senator Tyson, and those were the details you focused on. What you didn't see in a few the shots you'd taken were other people. Other people who weren't important to you because you were focused on the man chained in the center of the compound. You'd been following the rumors about an American being held, and when you found him, you mentally zeroed in on him—but your camera was looking at a much larger picture."

Brock saw Mia's blue eyes flicker with understanding, and he could practically hear the whirl of her thoughts as comprehension washed over her. Cam must have seen the same response because he smiled at her indulgently.

"I do so love that spark of intelligence in a woman's beautiful eyes. I see that in my lovely pet's eyes all the time, and it fills me with pride knowing the brilliant woman behind those sparkling eyes belongs to me. Your Masters are very lucky men, Mia."

Cam's compliment sent a pretty pink stain over her cheeks, but some of the tension drained from her muscles, and Brock knew that had been part of Cam's goal. Cameron Barnes could be a ruthless son of a bitch, but he was also a seasoned operator and interrogator who knew the value of a few well-placed words of praise.

"Are you saying I took pictures of someone who is worried enough about being exposed, they'd hurt my grandfather?"

"Not exactly. We believe General Moreno was responsible for poisoning your grandfather, and we believe he has a different motive for wanting to keep you close."

Mia's entire body went deathly still. Hell, she even stopped breathing until Brock leaned close and said, "Breathe, baby."

Everyone on the team agreed there was something amiss between Mia and the man charged with her family's security, but so far, they hadn't been able to find any clues what the problem might be. If the retired general had pressured Mia for a romantic relationship, Brock wasn't sure he'd be able to hold Tucker back, but his gut told him that wasn't the real issue between them.

"I'll kill the pickle licker with my bare hands," Mia's response startled everyone in the room except for her new friend whose roar of laughter earned her an embarrassed smile from Mia.

"Damn, I like her so much. Can we keep her, Master?" CeCe's sweet words brought chuckles from around the room. Cam's indulgent smile as he pulled CeCe down for a quick kiss gave everyone a chance to take a breath.

"It's a lovely idea, pet, but I've gotten the idea Brock and Tucker might have other plans for her."

Damned straight, we do.

MIA HADN'T BEEN kidding about wanting to wrap her hands around Joseph Moreno's wrinkled throat. The only problem was it would require her to get closer to him than she ever intended to be. Maybe she'd use a baseball bat. Although that wouldn't allow her to feel his struggle to breathe. Damn, her fiery temper was going to get her in trouble if she wasn't careful.

When Tucker turned to her, his green eyes were so pale with anger, she instinctively leaned away from him. His hard expression softened immediately, and she knew he hadn't been angry with her but had simply picked up on her own powerful emotions.

"I'll kill him myself if he hurts you, sweet cheeks. There won't be a hole on this planet deep enough for him to hide in. Later, we're going to be asking a lot of questions about why you don't trust him, but right now we have bigger fish to fry."

She remembered reading an article once about American slang and their strange expressions, but she didn't recall anything being mentioned about cooking fish. Before she could ask, CeCe spoke up.

"Bigger problems." Mia's expression must have given away her confusion, because CeCe added, "The fish fry thing... it means there are bigger problems to deal with first. Don't ask me why, but most southern expressions involve food or sports."

Mia made a mental note to do a little research later on

southern expressions. If she was going to Texas, it would be useful to speak the language... and evidently, English wasn't the only language spoken there. Giving CeCe a quick nod of thanks, she turned her attention back to Cam.

"Okay, what other fish are you planning to fry?"

His entire expression shifted between one second and the next, and Mia felt the photographer in her sit up and take notice. God in heaven, how she would love to capture that fleeting expression on film. She'd gotten a glimpse of a much younger and more carefree man than the one who'd been studying her so closely every time they'd met. The man she'd seen so briefly was fun loving and overflowing with intellectual curiosity. He loved learning for the simple joy of discovering new things. And before she could stop her train of thought, Mia knew those were the same things she'd seen in Brock and Tucker's eyes when they'd made love to her the night before.

"I'm not sure I've ever had a woman look at me with that particular expression. If I'm not mistaken, that's the look of an artist assessing how to freeze a moment in time," Cam's quietly spoken words pulled her out her thoughts, and she nodded.

"Sorry, professional hazard. Now, can you explain what you saw in the pictures?"

One of the men leaning against the wall stood to his full height, stepped forward, and smiled at her. "I'm Micah Drake. I work for Kent and Kyle West."

"Meet the Prairie Winds Club's computer wizard." CeCe's brilliant smile told her she had a tremendous amount of respect for the man tapping on his phone's keyboard.

"I'm not sure about the wizard part, but I appreciate your vote of confidence, CeCe."

The man looked more like a surfer than a computer expert, but she wasn't fooled by his casual stance. There was a will of pure iron lurking behind those crystal blue eyes. Damn, she wished she'd had time to do her homework on the people who worked for Prairie Winds. She hated being behind the information curve.

"Were you already on the ship when I arrived? I don't remember seeing you before. I don't always remember everyone, but I wouldn't have missed you because you look like one of those singers. The ones who sing the beach songs." CeCe's snicker let Mia know she'd understood who Mia was referring to, but the scowling look on Tucker's face wasn't as reassuring. Who knew he'd have such a negative reaction to a singing group.

"No, I flew in this morning to speak with you personally." His matter-of-fact tone was edged with something she wasn't able to identify, and she wasn't going to try. He walked over to what looked like a large television at the side of the room. With a few taps on his phone, the screen brightened with what she recognized as the encampment where Senator Tyson was being held. "I can tell by your expression you recognize the location." She nodded and moved to stand in front of the screen.

"I don't know what you've done to the shot, but I want you to teach me how to do it. Holy candlesticks, this is amazing. The detail is astonishing. Look at the delicate shadows highlighting the veins of the leaves. And the way the backlight filters through the jungle canopy, etching an added dimension to what was already a long-range picture." It was hard to resist tracing the changes with her fingers, the enhancements were truly remarkable. When she finally looked back to Micah Drake, he was smiling indulgently.

"I'll be happy to show you how to enhance your pictures although we'll have to highjack the software since the program I used isn't available on the commercial market. I promise you, Phoenix Morgan will be happy to barter with you, he has a young daughter who seems to delight in terrorizing photographers." She couldn't hold back her laughter. Mia seemed to have a gift for taking pictures of children and enjoyed it when she had the time.

"I'll keep that in mind. I think I'm up to the challenge, and I'm certain it would be worth the trouble. This is amazing."

"It isn't hard when the photographs are this crisp. You're very talented, Ms. Mendez. Now, I want you to turn your attention to the people in the picture. Do you recognize any of them?"

Chapter Sixteen

Tucker didn't know what had come over him when Mia compared Micah to one of the Beach Boys. She hadn't been flirting, but for a few seconds he'd flashed back to the witch he'd been married to, and all the anger and jealousy had boiled to the surface before Brock's scathing glare brought him back to his senses.

Watching her scrutinize the photo, he'd seen Mia's admiration for what Micah had done to enhance the detail. Their interaction had been purely professional, and he was ashamed of his earlier reaction. Watching her study the men standing in the background of the photo, Tuck could see her concentrate on each figure before moving to the next. When her gaze landed on the man they were most interested in, he saw her eyes widen in surprise before her brows drew together in a frown.

"Who is this? He doesn't fit here."

No shit. It was like one of those picture puzzles you saw in a children's magazine. Which one of these things is not like the other?

"You're right. He doesn't fit. Tell me what you see." Micah hadn't moved, and his words were coaxing rather than commanding. The team wanted to tap into her photographer's eye, and he had to give Micah credit for getting there so effectively. This was the reason Kyle West had insisted on flying the head of Prairie Winds security to the ship rather than waiting a few days for her to arrive on site.

"He's wearing a suit. Who wears a suit in the jungle? His shoes are wrong. The clothes are wrong and... oh shit, he's looking right at the camera."

Tucker watched the blood drain from her pretty face, and she swayed. His feet were already moving before his mind processed the need, and he pulled her into his arms and waited for Brock to slide a chair behind her. Once she was seated, Tucker pressed a quick kiss to her forehead and motioned for her to continue.

"So... does this means the rumors I heard about your government being involved are true?"

Tucker was impressed. She hadn't missed a beat, assessing the situation in a few seconds and drawing the same conclusion they had after a damned hour-long meeting.

Cam stepped forward and nodded. "I think you're right. The man you captured in the photograph works for a shadow agency within the CIA."

"What does that mean, exactly?"

"Technically, it means he doesn't exist. But, that being said, I think his clothing is a clue. Let's take a closer look." Micah tapped in a quick command, and the next picture came up zooming in on the man in question. "Do you recognize him, Mia?"

Everyone in the room knew the answer before she had the chance to respond. Her expression reflected recognition almost immediately.

"Yes. He works at one of my grandfather's banks. He started about a year or so ago in a branch that wasn't doing very well, but from what I've heard, it's made a remarkable recovery under his leadership." Tucker saw her hands begin to tremble and knew she was piecing things together.

"Oh, fudge. My grandfather is going to go insane when he hears this."

Tucker wasn't worried about her grandfather's frustration at being infiltrated, but he was damned worried about Mia's safety. The man in the photo was going to use any means necessary to make sure he wasn't connected to Tyson's captivity. There wasn't anyone in the world more dangerous than a covert operator on the cusp of being exposed in the midst of a black op because they had nothing to lose. The whole thing was an international incident in the making.

Four hours later, Mia sagged back in her chair, and Tucker finally gave into temptation and lifted her into his arms and stalked to the door. She'd been grilled about every detail in the photos, the rumors she'd heard, and Tyson's escape. Micah and Cam had used every interrogation trick in the book and some Tucker wondered if they hadn't made up on the spot. The only reprieve she'd gotten was the brief FaceTime call with Tally Tyson who'd thanked Mia for the photos and promised they'd meet personally as soon as possible.

"She's had enough. The rest can wait until she's been fed and gotten some rest." Tucker had seen Cam go days without any significant rest, but he wasn't going to stand by and watch him push Mia to the same point of exhaustion. Before the door closed behind him, he heard Cam's amused voice.

"Well, that didn't take as long as I thought it might. Good to see the fire back in his eyes." Tucker resisted the urge to return and tell his friend to go fuck himself, but it wasn't easy.

BROCK WATCHED HIS brother walk out with Mia cradled in his arms and felt a surge of hope, but it was also tinged with frustration. Turning back to Cameron Barnes and Micah Drake, Brock leaned back in his chair and watched them for several long minutes before speaking.

"Start talking." This was the first time Brock could remember seeing Cam visibly uncomfortable—hell, he was known for his cool detachment during even the diciest operations.

Micah leaned back against a table with his ankles and arms crossed in front of him. Brock noticed the dark circles under his eyes and wondered how long it had been since he'd rested. It was obvious he'd been working furiously gathering information. Everyone on the Prairie Winds team knew Micah was the go-to man for intel. Brock suspected government contacts used him when their legitimate resources weren't enough.

"Mia confirmed everything we've been hearing for months," Cam finally broke the silence. "Every rumor she mentioned and a few that probably hadn't filtered that far down. Her memory and attention to detail are remarkable, Kyle will probably try to hire her." Cam grinned at Micah, who nodded in agreement. The thought of Mia on an op sent a spike of fear through Brock's chest.

"Senator Tyson needs to surface—and he needs to do it damned fast or the cartel will cut their losses. There's no question the man working in Mendez's bank is playing both sides against the middle. He's laundering money and skimming. If he was in the U.S., he'd have already been caught, but banking in Colombia isn't regulated as closely."

Brock wasn't interested in the damned laws governing Colombian financial institution and he hoped his impatience showed.

Micah tapped a command into his phone and another picture appeared on the screen. This one showed two men watching from the shadows as he and Tucker escorted Mia along the dock.

"So, they knew where we were all along?" If that was true why hadn't they tried to stop her?

"These men work for Lucia." Cam's use of Mia's grandfather's first name implied they were closer than former acquaintances. "Not everyone on General Moreno's team is loyal to him, some of them are loyal to their boss—as they should be. They've had to shut down each time she's tried to leave the country, and from what I've heard, they were happy to sit this one out." The gleam in Cam's eyes meant the guys had probably already been paid off before they arrived with Mia. The man never ceased to amaze him.

"Where is Tyson being held, and who's calling the shots?" They'd been sent to Colombia to find out what Mia knew and retrieve the senator, and Brock had to keep reminding himself the second part of that mission still hadn't been achieved.

"He's being held in a hotel in Medellin. Ironically, it's not far from the hospital Mendez is in. I swear the whole damned country operates in a four-block radius. Christ, it's worse than a small town. Everybody is up in everybody else's businesses." When they all blinked in surprise at Micah's outburst, he rubbed his hand over his face in obvious frustration.

"Shit. Sorry, but the more I learn about this mess, the less I seem to know. Phoenix is just as baffled, and I would have sworn that wasn't possible."

Brock agreed, Phoenix Morgan was one of the smartest men in the country. He'd made his first million while in high school, writing programs for games and completed college when most people were still trying to figure out where the student union was during Rush Week. If Micah and Phoenix hadn't figured out who was who in this zoo, Brock didn't stand a chance.

"If we know where Tyson is, why aren't we pulling him out?" Brock suspected he already knew the answer, but he wanted to hear their confirmation.

"We need to be damned sure what we're walking into. Everyone who knows Karl believes he's a victim. If he's suffering from Stockholm Syndrome, he might not be willing to leave." Micah looked at Cam, who shrugged. "Cam isn't as trusting, and with his experience, no one is willing to discount his opinion."

"Damn," Cam chuckled, "he makes me sound like a skeptical bastard, doesn't he?"

"And that, gentlemen, is my cue." CeCe stood up and shook her head. "I'm going to relax by the pool and drink something decadent and filled with all the goodies I won't be able to have if all goes according to plan."

Brock watched as she kissed both of her husbands and walked out. He also knew he shouldn't waste any time getting the information he wanted because neither Cam nor Carl would leave their spirited wife unattended for long.

With the door once again closed, Cam leaned back and propped his feet on the desk.

"I think there are other possibilities. Don't discount the possibility the man was in bed with one faction of the cartel before arriving and was held by an opposing group." When

Brock raised his brows, Cam held up his hand. "I'm not convinced that's the case, but I think it's something which bears consideration. I know the team discussed this contingency, and I don't have anything to add to their previous information. I just want all the cards on the table."

Carl leaned forward and flipped through a folder before speaking. "Have you considered mind altering drugs? Maybe he's being drugged and prepped before a pseudo-rescue by the same group holding him. With his political aspirations, he'd be a damned powerful ally as a senator and exponentially more valuable if he becomes President."

Micah shrugged. "I called Joelle Morgan and Merilee Lanham. Both women have extensive backgrounds in pharmaceuticals." *No shit.* Joelle recently won a Nobel prize for her work with the drugs used for cancer treatment. And Merilee was the Chief Executive Officer of a medical center, she had her ear to the ground on all the latest mind-altering drugs. "They've given me an extensive list of possible drugs and a very short list of facilities with the confidential resources to help if this is the problem."

Brock waited for several seconds and when no one else spoke up, he decided to say what no one else wanted to.

"And what's the plan if you find out he's dirty? What happens if your surveillance shows he's complicit?" Micah was the only one who knew the Senator well enough to count him as a friend, and he saw the man flinch ever so slightly at the blunt questions.

"We'll walk away. The pictures will disappear because no one wants to further endanger Mia even though I'd love to leak them to a few of my contacts to keep the pressure on the rogue operator, but I suspect Lucia Mendez and the cartel will take care of the problem."

"Timeline?" Brock hoped they wouldn't attempt a rescue until Mia was safely ensconced at Prairie Winds.

"They're still watching, but there's been some unusual activity at the hotel in the last couple of hours, so the team is on standby. We're docking in Cozumel tomorrow to avoid drawing unwanted attention by changing our itinerary. There are already guests asking about your presence and the chopper landing on the deck early this morning. Why anyone was up at the ass crack of dawn I don't know, but there you have it."

Brock laughed at Cam's frustration. After a career in Black Ops followed by years owning and operating a kink club, Cam Barnes was a sworn night owl. His dislike for dawn was well known.

Micah rolled his eyes. "In case anyone asks, I'm a real estate agent Mr. Barnes summoned because he doesn't have the fucking patience to wait until docking in Texas to see what properties are available between Houston and Austin. I think it's a brilliant cover because everyone knows he has the patience of a gnat."

"Fuck you, Drake," Cam's laughter defied his harsh words, and Micah just shrugged because everyone knew what he'd said was the truth.

Brock shook his head and headed for the door. "Keep us posted. I want to check on Mia, you asshats badgered her into exhaustion. If you fucked up our plans for tonight, I'll shoot you with your own guns and throw your disrespectful asses overboard." The last thing he heard as the door closed behind him was their taunts and howling laughter. *Arrogant fuckers.*

Chapter Seventeen

TALLY TOSSED A discarded stack of papers into the trash and wiped the sweat from her brow with the back of her sleeve.

"It has to be here. I know I saw it, and he never threw anything away... fucking pack rat. Who needs all this stuff, and why the hell didn't I throw it away months ago? There's a question Freud would have a field day with."

She'd been sorting through Karl's old files for hours, determined to find a letter she remembered seeing laying on the kitchen counter a few days before her husband's ill-fated trip to Colombia. The envelope had been an odd size, and the flowing script so beautiful, it stood out. She'd planned to ask him about it, but an emergency call back to the hospital had taken precedence.

The damned thing had completely slipped her mind until early this morning, and she'd been on a tear ever since. She'd been cursing herself for keeping all Karl's stuff, but now she wondered if her subconscious hadn't been trying to remind her about the letter. Looking at her watch, Tally was shocked to see it was almost four o'clock in the afternoon. She'd hauled out bag after bag of shredded paper, but she only had one more box to sort. There was finally light at the end of this paperwork tunnel.

"If he comes back here and saves one more piece of worthless paper, I swear I'll burn the damned house down."

Grabbing the last box, Tally settled on the floor close to the overworked shredder and pulled the lid from the box. Her eyes widened in surprise when she realized these were the most recent postmarks she'd seen. Some of these envelopes were dated after Karl's disappearance, which meant someone else had boxed up the contents. There had been a lot of people in and out of the house during the first couple of months, so it was likely one of her friends had been trying to help and taken it upon themselves to store these away. For the first time, Tally felt a surge of hope she might find what she was looking for. She wasn't sure why, but something told her that envelope was a clue, and she was past ready to find out if her husband had walked away from her willingly or if he was a pawn in some government agency's twisted game of chess.

KOI LEANED BACK in the leather chair he'd purchased for Tally's home office and watched the screen of his laptop as she rifled through box after box of trash. What Karl had been thinking keeping all that crap was a mystery to him. The truth was he and Tally were a much better fit than she and Karl had ever been, and her husband had known it. Koi knew from his first encounter with Karl, the man wasn't happy in their marriage, no matter how hard he'd tried to disguise his detachment.

Everyone he'd talked to after the senator's disappearance had insisted their differences had only become a problem when he'd begun pressuring her to move back to Washington. The one exception had come from a woman he'd least expected.

Several months ago, Koi had been in Texas on business and had run into Brinn Peters. The young woman had stirred up a lot of trouble at Mountain Mastery, but she had been the one to call for help when he'd been badly injured in a car accident. It was no exaggeration to say she'd saved his life that night, and for that, he'd be forever grateful. He'd stopped to talk with her while she and her Doms shared dinner at a local restaurant. Brinn had looked so different from the high-strung woman he'd met in Montana, he might not have recognized her if she hadn't spoken to him as he walked past.

She'd introduced him to Parker Andrews, who he already knew was the local Police Chief, and Dan Deal, a psychologist with a successful practice in Austin. She'd asked him to convey her sympathy to Tally, then surprised him by commenting she hoped Tally could retain her sweet memories of her husband because the ache of shattered illusions was more painful than losing someone you thought you knew. They'd been interrupted by the waiter before he could question her, and then the moment was lost.

Twisting the slender, silver pen between his fingers, Koi knew what Tally was looking for because he'd been the one to tuck it in the bottom of the box of unrelated mail. His hope had been she wouldn't find it until she was strong enough to handle the contents—he sent up a silent prayer to his ancestors he'd made the right choice. That damned letter was going to change the way she viewed everything about her life before Karl's plane went down, and he hoped he had what it was going to take to put her heart back together again.

Koi hadn't pushed Tally to throw any of it away sooner because he'd known it was something she needed to do in her own time. Sighing, he was glad she hadn't heard him come in several hours ago, but he wasn't pleased knowing she hadn't taken a break or eaten anything all day. They'd be having a long chat about that soon enough.

When he saw she was getting close the bottom of the small box, he pushed out of the comfort of his chair and started making his way downstairs to the room where Karl Tyson's collection of unimportant papers had been stored. He'd carry out the last bags of shreds tomorrow. Tonight, the woman who'd captured his heart before she'd even said hello was going to need him, and he'd do whatever it took to help her deal with the firestorm of emotions he was sure was coming.

MIA FELT DRAINED. How could she be so tired when all she'd done was sit passively for hours answering questions? She'd been close to breaking before Micah Drake had let her talk with Tally. The other woman had assured her she appreciated Mia's consideration in sending the pictures to her directly instead of to the government, even if it had been a shock.

After sending the envelope of pictures, Mia had researched the young surgeon and knew she'd walked away from a lucrative future in Washington D.C. after meeting the popular senator from Montana. Everything she'd read indicated the other woman had fallen in love with her new home and had no desire to return to the east coast. Micah Drake had confirmed Karl Tyson's insistence Tally return to the nation's capital had been nearing the breaking point when he'd disappeared.

What would it be like to lose someone you'd been

ready to leave? Had Tally felt a measure of relief? Had Mia been responsible for ending that respite, or would she have found out, eventually? They would probably never know what might have been. From Mia's perspective, the whole thing reminded her of cartoons she'd seen as a child. Something as small as pushing a snowball down a mountain could have devastating consequences for those unsuspecting people along its path. What had started as her desire to chase a story had quickly changed everything in her life. And like all major changes... there were both good and bad pieces.

As she lay in Tucker's arms, she couldn't stop the flow of tears of compassion she felt for Tally. She'd been incredibly gracious, but she'd been unable to hide what Mia suspected was a deep sense of betrayal. Why hadn't Karl made some attempt to contact his wife? And why hadn't the U.S. government told her he was still alive? Questions whirled around in her mind until she was almost dizzy trying to keep track.

"You're thinking so hard, you're going to give *me* a headache," Tucker's teasing tone surprised her, and she raised her head to look at his profile. He always seemed so serious... almost to the point of being sad; she wanted to see what teasing Tucker looked like. Much to her surprise, he looked much younger, and the sparkle in his green eyes made her wonder if this was the way his family saw him.

"I'm sorry, I was just thinking about Tally. She was so sweet, but I could see the pain in her eyes, and it's hard knowing I had a part in putting it there."

Tucker didn't respond until they were inside their suite. He sat her on one of the bar stools and pulled her into his arms. For several minutes, he just held her without uttering a word. When he finally pulled back, she was surprised by the depth of compassion in his sparkling green eyes. This was a man who'd suffered, and she suspected he'd been as affected by Tally's grace under pressure as she'd been.

"You're a rare treasure, Mia. Most people wouldn't have seen Tally's pain. For what it's worth, I think you're right about everything except your misguided guilt. The rumors of Tyson's survival were gaining strength and credibility. The Wests were already talking about sending a team in, the pictures just upped their timeline. We'll wait for Brock to find out whatever they weren't saying, and trust me, Cam and Micah were wringing every last detail from you, but they weren't showing any of their own cards."

When she tensed, he shook his head and continued, "No, they weren't being asses, they didn't want to prejudice any of your answers by telling you what they knew. Witnesses integrate any information they're given into their minds... usually unconsciously, so they were simply trying to prevent that from happening. Don't get me wrong, that was an interrogation, a damned tough one, but we're all on the same team, and even if they didn't say so, they're grateful for your help.

"There is something familiar about Cameron Barnes, I'm sure we've met before, but every time I think I've figured out it out, a different name pops into my head." She'd been struggling with it since meeting him and unraveling the mystery was starting to become an obsession.

The same boyish grin she'd seen earlier transformed his entire expression into one she suddenly wanted to see more. She shook off the mental image of the Deitz brothers spending any time with her beyond delivering her into the

Wests' care as the fantasy it was. It hurt to know their interest was an illusion but accepting the truth later... after she'd fallen for them, would hurt a lot more.

"I don't know what just went through that pretty head of yours, but you need to shake it off and come back to me." Tucker's hands wrapped around the sides of her neck, his thumbs brushing along the underside of her jaw. His hold wasn't physically restrictive, but the psychological effect was undeniable. When he was satisfied he once again had her attention, Tucker gave her a knowing look.

"You are so beautiful and more responsive than we could have hoped for. Watching the pulse at the base of your neck accelerate and your dark eyes dilate makes me want to strip you and fuck you until I've chased those insecurities out of your mind. As for Cam, keep in mind the man is a master at disguise. He's known your grandfather for years. I'm sure you've met him any number of times, and it's unlikely he'd have ever been introduced to you as the same man twice."

Mia was speechless. It had never occurred to her that Cameron Barnes was an acquaintance of her grandfather's. The revelation shouldn't have surprised her as much as it did.

"Well, I guess this explains why you have been so willing to help me and why Mr. Barnes was willing to hold the ship until we arrived." She suddenly felt disillusioned. They already had the pictures, and now that she'd told them everything she knew, there was no reason for her to stay. When they docked in Cozumel tomorrow, she'd catch a flight to... She sucked in a breath and whispered, "Where will I go? I can't go home, and I don't have—"

The door of the suite slammed closed just as Tucker picked her up off the bar stool and set her on her feet. His scowl was her first clue her self-talk hadn't just been spoken in her mind.

"Why isn't she naked?" Brock's barked question behind her made Mia jump and spin around.

Clutching her chest, she gasped, "Ropes and lizards, you scared the cotton out of me," she gasped, clutching her chest.

"Our sub thinks the only reason we're helping her is because Cam is acquainted with her grandfather."

Brock's snort told her he didn't think much of her conclusion. She noticed he hadn't disagreed; evidently, he didn't like being confronted with the truth. Tucker crossed his massive arms, and she tried to not stare at the way his black t-shirt pulled tightly over his thick chest. The move molded the shirt to his abs, outlining his well-defined six-pack, and she hoped like hell she wasn't drooling. She'd been looking forward to running the tip of her tongue over each of those ridges, but fate seemed to have other ideas. His eyes blazed with a searing heat that stole her breath, and she knew she'd been caught lusting after his body.

"She's also planning to bolt since she thinks she's no longer needed."

"Oh, I see. Since we've wrung all the information from her, she thinks we're going to cast her aside. She doesn't have a very high opinion of us, does she?" Brock shifted a step closer, and she fought the temptation to take a step back. Without thinking, she glanced toward the door, silently trying to calculate her chances of beating them to the exit.

And then what, genius? I'm on a damned boat! It's not like I can catch a cab and disappear.

"I swear if she tries to run, I'm going to give every Dom on the boat two swats with the paddle of their choice," Tucker's growled threat made her wonder if he would really let another man touch her.

"Good plan. I don't want their hands on her bare ass, but if they use a paddle, they'll be able to make their point."

Tucker glared at her as Brock spoke, but there was a twinkle in his eye that showed he wasn't as angry as he sounded. But she didn't want any of the other Doms touching her... with anything. That was something she couldn't ever see herself allowing. Of course, she'd never envisioned herself having sex with two men at the same time, either. Maybe she didn't know herself as well as she believed.

"Strip," Brock's one-word command was such a surprise, she could only stare at him blinking for several seconds. Neither of them made a move toward her, simply watched as she tried to get her brain and body to work together.

Maybe a couple of good orgasms before I go? Sort of like a goodbye gift? Don't most people give watches or wine?

Tucker's lips twitched, and she felt her face flush with embarrassment. Grabbing the hem of the dress they'd given her to wear, she pulled it over her head and tossed it aside. The cool air from the air conditioning hit her nipples, making them tighten, drawing the men's attention which made her nipples pull into even tighter peaks. If they didn't stop staring, the damned things were going to get so long and narrow, they'd break off. Tucker brushed the back of his knuckles over the tip of her left breast and smiled when she sucked in a quick breath.

"These beauties are going to look spectacular in jeweled clamps."

"Emeralds. We'll buy emerald beads for the chains.

We'll fuck her in front of a mirror and watch the stones sway with each thrust," Brock's words heated her from the inside out, but before she could respond the ship rocked violently to the side, pitching her between the two men. Tucker's arm snaked out so fast, she didn't even see him move as he secured her to his side.

"What the fuck?" Tucker held her as they tilted the opposite direction, sending trinkets tumbling from the shelves, instantly turning the floor into an obstacle course of broken glass. Adding to the confusion was a shrill alarm sounding above their heads, and Mia instinctively burrowed into Tucker's chest and clasped her hands over her ears. She didn't know how he was staying on his feet, but she was grateful he was keeping her from bouncing around like a pea in a can.

Brock turned from the glass sliders to shout, "Storm! Get her dressed, we need to get mid-ship before it gets any worse."

She didn't have a lot of experience on boats, but she assumed the rocking would be less in the middle, and she was already starting to feel queasy. Minutes earlier she'd been hungry, but just thinking about eating now made her hiccup in an effort to stave off the growing feeling of nausea.

Tucker pulled her dress over her head before picking her up and sprinting down the hall.

"Hang on, sweet cheeks, it'll be much better when we get you moved into the center of the ship. This is one of the hazards of cruising the western Caribbean, the weather is fickle."

The closer they got to the middle of the small ship, the more her stomach settled.

"Why didn't it bother you? You caught me and didn't

even shift on your feet. And Brock moved to the doors without holding on to anything." The minute she asked the question, she slapped her hand over her forehead. "Oh geez, I can't believe I asked that." His chuckle made her smile.

"Yeah, this is nothing compared to riding squalls out in a Zodiac. Don't let the military blow smoke up your ass about shock mitigation. Those fuckers are rocket fast, they turn on a fucking dime, and they are going to rattle your teeth no matter how calm the sea."

He sat her between CeCe and another young woman she'd met earlier. *Laura*. Her husbands worked for Cam, one of them managed the club in Houston if Mia remembered correctly.

Tucker gave her a quick kiss and promised to return with a snack. She didn't know how he'd known she was hungry, but she was grateful. After he'd walked away, CeCe grinned.

"Eating is the best way to control motion sickness, and it usually helps with morning sickness as well." Mia must have looked as confused as she felt because CeCe laughed. "The last part was for future reference. From the way Tucker was looking at you, I'd say it won't be long until you can use that tidbit."

Chapter Eighteen

"THIS IS THE excuse we've been looking for gentlemen. We're going to detour around Cozumel and head for Houston." Brock understood why Cam was anxious to skip the party stop, but he wasn't entirely convinced this storm was a blessing.

"How far are we offshore?" Security at the popular port would have been a nightmare, and Brock was as anxious as anyone to get Mia to the safety of the Prairie Winds compound, but as a former SEAL, he also knew the value of executing an insertion during a storm. He didn't want to be a target as they skirted bad weather.

"Only a couple of miles, but we're angling a little closer to try to get ahead of the worst of the storm," Cam answered absently while studying a chart on his laptop.

"How is your surveillance equipment working?" Brock already knew the answer but wanted to make sure Cam was paying attention to the fact they wouldn't see an approaching boat until it was too fucking close.

Micah Drake was sitting nearby, typing furiously on a keyboard.

"We've already positioned people on the deck, but it's probably wasted effort since they can't see a damned thing. At this point, the storm is a bigger threat than someone coming aboard. Kyle is working to find out if there are any teams nearby Uncle Sam might be planning to send out to retrieve Mia."

"As soon as the Wests knew what we were facing, they ordered the rest of the team in Medellin to pull Tyson out." Cam was obviously playing offense rather than defense, and Brock breathed a sigh of relief. Anyone directing a team to pull Mia in was going to be too busy covering their own ass to focus on her—he hoped.

KARL TYSON HEARD shouting in the hall outside the suite he'd been locked in for what felt weeks, but with no access to anything remotely connected to the outside world, he had no way of knowing for sure how long it had been. When the shouts grew louder, he became concerned and wondered what the problem was.

The men charged with watching over him had been even more agitated than usual the past few days, and it seemed they'd redoubled their efforts to convince him the organization they worked for was a legitimate pharmaceutical company wanting nothing more than an equal opportunity in the open market of the United States.

Shaking his head, Karl tried to remember why that seemed wrong and why they insisted on telling him the same thing again and again. Anytime he tried to remember what his life had been like before this room, his head felt like it was going to explode. Pressing his fingers over his temples to ease the pain, Karl heard gunfire and quickly moved to the back of the large walk-in closet to hide. Without a weapon, he wouldn't stand a chance in a hand-to-hand battle. He'd been exercising whenever they left him alone for a few minutes, but he was still too weak to fight off anyone intent on hurting him.

Settling in the darkest corner of the closet, he heard the unmistakable sound of wood splintering, then shouts as the fight spilled into the suite. Karl sucked in a breath when he realized the voices were speaking English, and they didn't have the accent he'd grown accustomed to hearing whenever his captors tried to communicate with him in his native language. No—these were Americans, and Karl felt a surge of hope for the first time in so long, he was afraid to give it more than a passing thought.

There was a part of him that remembered all the prayers that had gone unanswered—all the dark nights he'd lay awake trying desperately to hold on to memories that now seemed beyond his grasp. He still didn't understand how he could remember wanting to hold on to the fragments of his mind while being unable to remember what those bits and pieces of his memory contained.

His days were filled with torment as he tried to sort through the jumbled images playing in his dreams and dancing just far enough out of his reach to steal his focus during the few hours each day he was awake enough to think at all. Where did all those lost hours go each day? What was he doing or what was being done to him? Harboring any hope he'd ever find his way back to his previous life seemed like little more than an exercise in frustration, and attempting to put it together in his mind resulted in headaches so severe, he often succumbed to the overwhelming nausea.

He wasn't sure how long he'd been wandering around lost in his own thoughts when the sound of heavy footsteps moving closer brought him back to the moment. Whoever was out there wasn't making any effort to hide their approach. A few seconds later, the closet door opened, and Karl found himself blinking at the bright light shining in his eyes.

"Senator Tyson, we're here to take you home." Sagging with relief, he wanted to weep.

He might not remember his previous life, but at this point, he had nothing to lose by putting himself in the stranger's care. Karl let the man help him to his feet.

"My name's Sam McCall. Come on, let's get the hell out of here before the locals show up and drop a net over us." Another soldier slid a pair of slippers on his feet, and they led him down a hallway that looked more like a war zone.

The men surrounding him were moving so fast, Karl was having trouble keeping up. Stepping over the bodies of several men he knew had been stationed outside his door, they moved quickly to the stairwell. The man who'd said his name was Sam must have sensed his reluctance because he turned and grasped Karl's upper arm. Looking down, he was shocked to see Sam's hand completely encircled his bicep.

"It's too dangerous to use the elevator. We've got to take the stairs. Do you think you can make it to the roof?"

Karl wasn't sure how close they were to the top of the building, but he was certain it couldn't be far. He didn't know how long he'd last running up several flights of stairs, but he was determined to try. Nodding, he preceded the man up the narrow stairway. He sagged in relief when he discovered he'd only had to sprint up four short flights before they burst through a heavy door, spilling out onto the roof.

A few yards ahead, a helicopter sat with its blades turning slowly. When Karl realized the woman sitting in the pilot's seat wasn't wearing a uniform like the men who surrounded him, he and drew up short. When he hesitated,

Sam leaned down to shout in his ear.

"That's my wife, Senator. She's a hell of a pilot, and you can bet your ass she's going to get us the hell out of Dodge." *Wife?* Sam didn't look familiar, but with his face partially covered it might be hard to tell. But the closer he got to the woman, the more he relaxed. She was smiling at them as they climbed in the back of the chopper and a series of images raced through his mind, but it was gone before he could make sense of it.

Any time he tried to piece the pictures together into a memory, it triggered violent headaches, so he silently pushed aside whatever made the young woman seem familiar. The last thing he wanted to do was begin vomiting in front of the men who'd risked their lives to rescue him.

The other men all smiled at him, offering him a helping hand, and handing him a bottle of water and a granola bar, but Sam was the only one who'd introduced himself. He was grateful he only had to remember one man's name because he wasn't sure he could have handled any more.

Leaning back, Karl let them fasten his seatbelt as a wave of exhaustion hit him with the strength of a tsunami. Closing his eyes, the last thing he remembered was the weightless feeling he recognized as the aircraft lifting quickly into the air.

SAM KNEW THE senator hadn't recognized him even though they'd met on several occasions—the camo paint probably hadn't helped. Tyson was little more than a shell of his former self, and the needle tracks on his arms confirmed one of the team's fears. He was definitely being drugged—

now the question was what they had been giving him and how long did they have to relocate him to a medical facility before he went into withdrawal? Sam watched the emaciated man sitting next to him take a couple of drinks from a bottle of water, then fall instantly asleep. Hell, they hadn't even gotten off the ground when his eyelids slid closed.

Karl Tyson had impressed the hell out of him by running up the stairs when it was obvious he was operating on nothing but pure adrenaline. The small stumble when he'd seen Jen was the only time he'd missed a step, and Sam didn't know many men who didn't react the same way when they laid eyes on his gorgeous wife.

Her long, pale blonde hair and crystal blue eyes were only eclipsed by her warm smile and colorful personality. Sam always cautioned people that judging Jen based on her appearance was a mistake, but they rarely listened—until they found themselves cut off at the knees by her Mensa-level intelligence and smart mouth. He and Sage had won a lot of bets doing little more than wagering how long she'd let an asshat treat her like an airhead before she lowered the boom on them.

Sam had been terrified when Jen announced she was going to learn to fly. There was a reason the team called her Miley—she was a five foot nothing wrecking ball when he and Sage weren't keeping her contained. But she'd tackled flight instruction with a single-minded purpose that shocked everyone. She'd been completely focused on becoming a pilot, and everyone agreed she had a natural affinity for it. Watching her maneuver the craft through the complicated air traffic control patterns of the city was damned impressive.

Once they were out of the city, it wouldn't take them long to fly to the small airstrip just outside the radar range of the Jose Maria Cordova International Airport. The team's small jet was waiting, ready to take off the minute they were on board. As a team leader, Sam had been thrilled when the Wests agreed to purchase a smaller, more maneuverable jet. And now, each team had a jet they used, and their members were responsible for keeping the aircraft stocked with the supplies they most often needed.

His communication device crackled to life, and Jen's sweet voice sounded in his ear.

"We'll be setting down in ten. Our next ride is ready and waiting. The big bosses sent in a pilot, they seem to think I'm tired for some reason. You wouldn't know where they got such a strange idea, would you?"

Damn straight, he knew. He'd sent Kyle and Kent both messages asking for a relief pilot. Jen had been on standby for days, had taken shifts watching the hotel, and only slept in three- and four-hour increments since they'd gone wheels up in Texas ten days ago. He smiled because he knew she'd directed the question to him without opening her mic to the other members of the team.

"I promise to answer that question the next time you're naked and underneath me, doll. Now, get us to that damn jet, so we can get on our way. The sooner we deliver the good senator to the clinic, the sooner you'll get your answer."

He and Sage always made certain one of them had a line of sight on their sweet wife anytime she was flying. Sage was usually seated next to her since he was qualified to co-pilot all the aircraft they used. She turned briefly to look at him over her shoulder, flashing him a look filled with heat and promise. Damn, he was going to have to start pressing his bosses to overhaul the jet. *This thing needs a bedroom.*

Chapter Nineteen

MIA FLOATED ON the fringes of sleep, warm and comfortable as she listened to the steady beat of a heart beneath her ear. There were background noises, but she pushed them aside, content to let the steady thud lull her back into the erotic dream she'd been enjoying before the voices intruded. She'd been riding Tucker's thick cock, lifting herself up until the hard ring surrounding the head was teasing her vaginal opening before dropping back down, quickly taking him as deep as possible. She'd experimented until she found the angle that perfectly aligned with her G-spot, sending white-hot streaks of desire to every nerve ending with each stroke.

She knew she was dreaming… or at least she thought she was dreaming, but it didn't matter, the sensations were real enough to make her body respond. *Why is it so hot in here? I thought this ship had air conditioning. Why am I on a ship again? Cheese and crackers that feels so good.*

Her dream kept getting better and better because now Brock's voice was coming over her shoulder, and she felt his palms grip the cheeks of her ass. The calloused pads of his thumbs traced lines on either side of her crack.

"Such a beautiful ass, baby. I'm going to enjoy pushing my cock past this tiny rosette."

The cool drizzle of lube snaking down to coat the tight ring of muscles sent a shiver of need through her. Having both men buried deep in her was going to be a dream come true.

"Please. I want to feel you both inside me." The beat of Tucker's heart accelerated, and in the convoluted thinking of her dream, Mia wondered if he was having the same fantasy. Brock's finger circled her anus, massaging the lube deeper with each pass until the tip of his digit pressed against the tight ring. "It hurts so good. Oh, please don't stop."

As her mind cleared of the fog, she accepted this wasn't a dream at all. She'd been floating in a space she'd only read about in the novels on her electronic reader. Donut holes, those books were sorely lacking in their description of the haze of endorphins. The authors she favored needed to step up their game.

"I think our sub is starting to come back down, let's spin her up again before I fuck this sweet ass."

Brock's voice was rough with arousal, and Mia hoped he and Tucker were as affected as she was. *I sure don't want to be the only one getting lost in all this.* She'd promised herself she wouldn't fall for Brock and Tucker, but they were making it impossible to keep her distance.

"I swear she can drift off faster than any woman I've ever known."

"Makes you appreciate Kent and Kyle's frustration with Tobi, doesn't it? The two of them will probably be great friends." Mia forced her eyes open far enough to see Tucker's wicked grin. "Welcome back, sweet cheeks. Enjoying your ride?"

Was she ever.

TUCKER WISHED HE'D listened to the voice in his head that had encouraged him to bow out of the public scene they'd planned and stayed in their suite. The intimacy he'd originally hoped to keep at arm's length was now something he wanted to savor. He was a selfish bastard and wanted to keep it between the three of them. Sharing Mia's passion with everyone gathered around the stage frustrated him, and he worried she'd feel used rather than fulfilled tomorrow when she had time to consider the consequences of what she'd done.

He'd persuaded Brock to move the scene to one of the smaller stages where the seating was limited to just a few people. So far, Mia hadn't seemed affected one way or the other, but he'd seen subs freak out when the reality of having sex in front of other people finally hit them. Even the most experienced Dom could be blindsided by a submissive's sudden meltdown. Hell, he'd known more than one sub who'd walked away from the lifestyle without ever looking back after coming apart in public.

Banding his arms around her, Tucker held her against his chest and tried to slow his breathing. Before he'd sent her over the first time, they'd played with her enough to wind her up pretty tight, but he'd still been shocked to see the glaze of sub-space clouding her dark eyes. Knowing she'd slipped into that state of euphoria so easily was a major turn on. His cock throbbed inside her as he remembered how her body had almost floated off the spanking bench she'd been strapped over.

Mia might well be the most natural submissive he'd ever topped. He'd recognized it the first time he'd looked into her dark chocolate eyes. She was the perfect example of the *two sides of the same coin* explanation of submission. Mia was a gifted photographer with great instincts for identifying a relevant photo-op before the issue became newsworthy. She was also self-aware enough to know she wouldn't thrive working in one of her grandfather's banks. He admired the hell out of her for holding her ground against what must be tremendous pressure to buckle under and conform.

Listening to her soft sighs and muted groans of pleasure as they tried a variety of toys, gauging her reactions to sensation play, Tucker had struggled to tame the beast scratching at the surface wanting to claim her in ways that would make his Sunday School teachers blush. Taking a deep breath, he tried to refocus his attention on anything but the exquisite feeling of Mia's pussy clenching his cock so tight, he kept sucking in deep breaths to keep from coming.

Reciting multiplication tables wasn't cutting it, so he began mentally reviewing the unanswered messages he knew awaited his return home. No doubt the menace he and Brock called a younger sister would have sent her share of texts and left any number of voice mail messages asking for help with some imagined dire emergency.

He loved her, but he didn't even want to think about how much extortion money he and Brock had paid the little demon over the years buying her silence. Keeping her quiet after she'd learned they were members of Dark Desires had been damned expensive. The jackass who'd told her was now banned for life—Cam hadn't been pleased. Nellora Deitz had always been hell on wheels, but once she'd gone to college, they'd stopped paying for her silence.

When thoughts of his damned sister weren't enough to distract him, Tucker was forced to admit there probably wasn't anything that could keep him from becoming lost in the feeling of her tight vaginal walls rippling around him. Fuck, the heat alone was destroying him. Brock's rough voice finally pushed into his awareness.

"Push back against me, baby. That's it, nice and slow."

Tucker was slouched in a chair with Mia impaled on his cock as he held her loosely in his arms. She was arching her back to push back to open herself to Brock's intrusion, and in turn, she was grinding her hard, little clit against him, ramping up her heat even further. When he felt her tense, Tucker knew Brock was close to pushing the widest part of his cock through the tight ring of muscles guarding her rear entrance. Slipping his hands between them, Tucker rolled her nipples between his fingers and gave them a quick pinch. The flash of pain was enough to distract her, and he heard Brock groan as he pushed in to the hilt.

"Fuck, baby. You're shredding my self-control. *Mine.*" Brock's growled claim didn't set off alarms in Tucker like it would have a few days ago. Hell, maybe he was finally putting the past behind him. "Tuck, now or never, brother. She's pushed me as far as I can go."

Tucker nodded and flexed his hips, pulling himself out until only the tip of his cock was still surrounded by her warmth. They set a steady pace of alternating thrusts, making sure one of them was filling her at all times.

"Oh, my dancing stars and galloping garters. It feels sooo good. So amazing. I'm going to come. I can't hold it back. *Please.*"

They hadn't told her she couldn't come, but obviously, her extensive reading list had taught her more than they realized. Tucker cupped the sides of her face and gave her the command she'd been waiting for.

"Come for us, Mia. Let's dance with those stars you're

talking about, love." If his own mind hadn't been tumbling ass over tea kettle, Tucker might have questioned the change of her pet name, but with his consciousness exploding into a fine mist, it didn't matter. He felt his seed burst into the condom and knew the minute the latex gave way. Struggling to keep Mia close, his mind raced as the possible outcomes streamed through his mind.

The first thing he had to do was take care of the woman laying over him like the softest cashmere blanket. There would be time later to tell her their lives might have just taken a dramatic turn, but that wasn't a conversation he wanted to have while other people slowly filtered away from the small area where they'd just shared an amazing ménage experience.

MIA WAS CONVINCED her mind would never be whole again. *Humpty-Fucking-Dumpty has nothing on me. I don't know anything about the king's horses or men, but they'll never find all the pieces anyway, so what's the point?*

Sex before she'd met Brock and Tucker had been so lackluster, she'd decided it wasn't worth the effort. Relying on her battery-operated-boyfriends to relieve the ache had been perfectly fine. Now? Well, now she was certain there would never be a device capable of pushing her to the point of no return. She didn't think a device had been invented that could provide a suitable substitute for the out-of-body experience she'd just experienced.

She wasn't sure how long she'd been mentally vacant, but when her brain finally kicked into gear, she was surprised to discover she'd been moved to the center of the bed in their suite. She suspected they'd once again cleaned and dried her pink bits because the messy feeling she vaguely remembered when Tucker pulled himself from her body was gone. Now she was surrounded by warmth... too much warmth.

Holy hellfires, she was going to burn to a crisp if she didn't get out from between these two. A mental cartoon where she popped up from between them looking like a scorched toaster pastry played in her head, and Mia had to fight back a giggle. Great... evidently, the strain of holding back her laughter was too much effort for her lazy bladder, now she had to use the restroom. Extricating herself from between Brock and Tucker without waking them was no easy feat, and when she was finally successful, Mia fought the urge to happy dance herself into the attached bathroom.

Walking out of the bathroom, her stomach growled so loud, she could have sworn the sound echoed through the large room. Both men stirred, and she froze in place, hoping they wouldn't wake up to discover she'd moved from between them. In the books she'd read, the Doms always seemed to be annoyed when their subs left the bed without permission. Smiling to herself and shaking her head, Mia still didn't fully understand it, and it was the one part of the stories she'd loved so much that always seemed over the top.

Grabbing a shirt and a pair of shorts from her bag, Mia went in search of food. It shouldn't be hard to find something to eat, right? Cruise ships are supposed to be twenty-four-hour floating restaurants according to the advertisements she'd seen.

The sound of the door latching behind her was almost deafening because she knew instantly, she was busted. Without a keycard, there was no way for her to get back into the suite. *Son of a biscuit, I really suck at this spy-game stuff.*

Twenty minutes later, she'd indulged in two large slices of the greasiest pepperoni pizza she'd ever eaten... damn, it had been good. Leaning on the rail, sipping her tea, Mia watched the water sluice by as the ship cut through the waves. She could see the flashes of lightning in the distance and was grateful they'd been able to skirt the storm even though some of the younger passengers had seemed disappointed with their change of course.

The steady slap of the waves against the hull was starting to lull her to sleep when she noticed a small light, not far from the ship. It seemed to be getting closer, but she couldn't be sure... frackleberry, distance was hard to judge over water, and she didn't have any real experience with anything remotely naval. The closer it came, the larger the light appeared, and she was shocked when it suddenly disappeared. Leaning forward, she wondered if she'd been hallucinating... probably. *Serves you right for eating greasy food in the middle of the night.*

Straining her eyes, Mia saw a flash of light a split second before being blindsided by what felt like a growling freight train. Her first instinct was to suck in a deep breath because she honestly thought she was being knocked overboard, but strong arms surrounded her, and everything slowed, just like it did in the movies. She was rolled to the side, so she landed on whoever had tackled her at the same time her mind registered the second crack of a rifle and a high-pitched ping of a bullet hitting metal. The sound of a rifle shots blasted over the water at almost the same time, and the sudden awareness that someone was shooting at her filled her with panic.

Her fear for her own safety evaporated in the heat of

rage that followed, but the rage was quickly replaced with stark terror someone else would be hurt trying to help her. She'd never be able to live with herself if Brock or Tucker were hurt protecting her. Damn, why hadn't she considered all the lives she was endangering by getting on this ship? She wasn't ever this selfish. Scrambling to put distance between herself and her savior, her mind blanked of everything but the need to make certain she was the only one in danger. If she could just move away from the man holding her, she'd be able to keep him from being shot by mistake.

Chapter Twenty

BROCK WOKE UP when the electronic lock on the door to their suite engaged. He instinctively reached for the pistol he always kept within reach, the Glock already in his hand before he realized the woman who'd been sleeping between them was gone. How Mia had managed to slip undetected from between them was as puzzling as it was annoying, and right now, he was annoyed as hell.

"I swear, I'm going to tie her to the fucking bed the next time she saps all our strength." And there would be a next time because he wasn't letting her go. Nudging Tucker, Brock snarled, "Get up. Mia is on the prowl." Tucker was usually the lightest sleeper Brock knew, so it spoke volumes that he'd slept soundly enough for Mia to slip away unnoticed.

"What the fuck? How did she get out from between us? Christ, I haven't slept that hard in years." Tucker was already pulling on his boots, and Brock wanted to laugh at his brother's frustration because he didn't doubt for a minute their little sub was going to pay dearly for this one.

"I don't know how she did it or how she thinks she'll get away with it when she didn't take a keycard with her." When Tucker started to charge past him, Brock shook his head. "Let's see what she's up to before we run out of here like a couple of bulls in a china closet. I don't want to find out there is a perfectly good explanation and end up looking like an ass." With most women, it wouldn't matter to him one way or another, but Mia was different. She mattered. Brock watched his brother take a deep breath before nodding.

"You're right. I don't want to fuck this up, either. I know I said I was going to keep my distance, but she's getting to me in a way I didn't think would ever happen again." Brock knew how difficult that admission had been for his brother, but he was damned relieved to hear them.

"Come on, let's find out what she's up to, and remind me to buy some damned vitamins when we get home. I have a feeling we're both going to need them to keep up with her." Brock would eat fucking children's chewables if it meant he'd be able to keep up with the hot woman whose submissive nature was a perfect match for the two of them.

Twenty minutes later, they stood in the shadows watching as Mia used her finger to dab the last crumbs of pizza from her plate. She'd eaten two of the largest slices of pepperoni pizza Brock had ever seen. Hell, he wasn't sure he would have been able to eat that much pizza as quickly, and he was a lot bigger. As if he'd read Brock's mind, Tucker let loose a low whistle.

"Fuck me, I can't even eat that much, and she's just a little bit of a thing."

"She's not a thing, Caveman Jack." Brock didn't bother disguising his frustration. There were times he was convinced his brother was a throwback to another time.

"Well excuse me, I forgot you're the newly appointed Chief of PCBS Police." Tucker's indignation was humorous since their younger sister always fussed about them referring to her as a "little bit of a thing." Nell knew what they meant, but she rejoiced in any flaw she could find in their treatment of women, and she was particularly fond of giving Tucker seven kinds of hell. Brock kept hoping the two of them eventually admit how much they cared about one another, but so far, it was little more than a pipe dream.

"If you two are finished sniping at each other, we have a bogie off the port side. They are coming in so fast, they were too fucking close by the time they hit our radar." Cam's voice behind them caused Brock and Tucker to jump. *Once a spook, always a spook—the damned man moves like a soft breeze.* Cam shook his head at them, a wry grin tipping the corners of his mouth in amusement.

"Brock, you're with me. Tucker, I want you to get closer to her, but don't intercede until you're forced to. Let's see how this plays out. It seems odd that she just happens to show up on the Lido Deck at the same time we get company." Brock had to agree, it was damned coincidental, and he'd found coincidences were damned rare. Damned rare, indeed.

Tucker's eyes went ice cold, and he nodded before moving silently along the wall. The new position would make it easier for him to see any interaction between Mia and the speeding boat.

When she moved to stand at the ship's rail, Brock wasn't sure who he was the most frustrated with her for fooling them or him for believing her damsel in distress routine, but he didn't have time now to mull it over. Pushing back the need to put his fist through the nearest wall, he followed Cam up two flights of stairs and came to an abrupt stop.

"Jesus, man, do you always carry a fucking arsenal along when you go on vacation?" There were several weapons set out—several damned impressive weapons—

but it was the missile launcher that caught his eye. Looking at the military-grade, shoulder-held weapon to Cam, he couldn't believe what he was seeing. "Seriously?" He could only stare at the armaments with a mixture of shock and admiration. Cam's grin should have been concerning, but Brock was too busy staring at the array of weaponry to worry about the former agent's amused expression.

"What can I say? My family is important to me, and I believe in being prepared."

Yeah, Barnes, you're a regular boy-fucking-scout.

TUCKER TRIED TO rein in his temper because, despite the way the situation had first looked, Mia's expression was one of confusion rather than expectation. From his new position, he could see her face clearly in the starlight. She appeared to be looking at the boat, but from the way her eyes narrowed, and her head tilted to the side, he didn't think she knew for sure what she was seeing.

To the untrained eye, the small light bobbing up and down might not make sense, but as a former SEAL, he knew exactly what he was approaching. The inflatable currently flying over the water was running in virtual darkness, but that didn't keep him from identifying it. The only light was from a small penlight Tucker would bet was being used to illuminate some fools attempt to load a weapon. *Fucking amateurs.*

As soon as the light went out, Tucker pushed off the wall. He didn't know if it was instinct or years of training, but he *knew* what was coming. He was just a few feet from Mia when he saw the muzzle flash in his peripheral vision. Her eyes widened in confusion a split second before he hit her full force from the side. Wrapping his arms around her, he rotated in mid-air so his much larger body absorbed the force of the fall. He felt her jerk in his arms, but he didn't dare take time to explain. Without slowing, he continued to roll until she was sheltered safely beneath him.

"Stay down. Don't move until I tell you to." Tucker's gruff command went unanswered, but he knew she'd heard him because she went still in his hold—for a second, two tops.

"Get off me. Some son of a basket tried to shoot me. They'll shoot you if you try to protect me. I'll die a thousand deaths if they hurt you. Get off me, right now."

Tucker was grateful she was so small because she was already a fucking handful. How the hell could someone so petite wiggle so much? Wrapping his legs around hers, he squeezed tight, immobilizing her.

"Stop fighting me, Mia," he snarled out, speaking against the shell of her ear. "They don't have a shot if we stay down. Cam and Brock are above us, let them do what they love." When she started to argue, he kissed her ear. "Sweet cheeks, they live for this shit. Knowing Cam, he's got all kinds of great gizmos up there, and they'll have a fucking field day taking these jokers out." Before she could respond, Tuck felt her go limp in his hold.

He didn't have time to move them into a safer position before he heard the distinctive hiss of a missile above them, and he would have cheered if he hadn't been so worried about the lifeless woman in his arms. Two seconds later an explosion lit up the night sky. Whoever they were, they'd been loaded for bear and probably hadn't expected the vacationers to be well armed. Fuckers should have done their homework because they obviously didn't know Cameron Barnes.

The deck was immediately flooded with light and seeing the blood pooling around Mia sent a wave of nausea and panic through him. Shouting for help, Tucker heard CeCe Barnes yelling at someone to let her go, and within seconds, she was pushing him aside. What the hell was it with small women tonight? Clearly, he needed to ramp up his workout schedule if he was getting moved around so easily by little people.

THE SOUND OF a gun being fired had CeCe leaping from the bed before Carl could stop her. She was dressed, had her bag in hand, and was headed to the door when Carl threw his arm around her waist, lifting her from the ground. He knew this woman better than she knew herself, and from the airy sound of her voice and the jackrabbit beating of her heart beneath his arm, he knew she was functioning on pure adrenaline.

"Where do you think you're going, baby?"

"I heard gunfire. Someone could need my help."

She hadn't even had time to come fully awake yet. They'd been down this path before, and he knew the doctor side of her brain was functioning perfectly, but the safety side wouldn't kick in for a while yet. It was his job to make sure she was safe—she didn't always appreciate what she called their high-handed, micromanagement of her schedule. Carl didn't give a rat's ass, and Cam cared even less. When it came to their family's safety—nothing was more important.

"You may be right but rushing headlong into a situation we know nothing about isn't going to help anyone. Let me lead, and we'll find out what's happening before we barge into something we aren't prepared for." He'd heard the missile launch and explosion, so there was little doubt the situation had been contained, but he wasn't going to take any chances.

Moving silently down the corridor, Carl heard Tucker's call for help at the same time the other man came into their view. Tuck was sheltering Mia's lifeless form as blood pooled beneath them. CeCe darted around him like a fucking rocket and was shoving Tuck aside before Carl could get his hands on her to hold her back.

"Fuck. I'd paddle your ass for that, but I know you'd like it."

He stood back and watched her work, still amazed at her ability to hit the ground running. Because the cruise had been for CeCe, many of her friends were also medical professionals, and as they began filtering out into the open area, every one of them pitched in to help. When Cam stepped up beside him, Carl smiled at the excited look in his lover's eyes.

"You look pleased with yourself."

"You have no fucking idea. Not only did I get to vaporize the fucker who shot Mia, but I got to do it in grand style. I'd like to say it wasn't fun, but why lie?" Cam was usually one of the least excitable people Carl had ever known, so seeing him lit from the inside with excitement was hot as hell. When Cam's eyes met his, they went from amused to smoldering between one blink and the next.

Cameron Barnes was the only man Carl had ever wanted. There had been other women in his life before he'd met Cecelia, but there'd never been any other man. The promise in Cam's eyes shot a bolt of heat to Carl's cock, and he was forced to shift his stance or risk a permanent zipper tattoo.

The heated moment between them was broken when CeCe shouted a question about their distance from Houston. Cam returned his attention to her.

"We'll dock in a couple of hours, pet, but the chopper Micah used is still on board if you need it." Moving closer, Carl looked at Tucker Deitz and was shocked to see the depth of emotion in the other man's eyes.

He'd known Tuck for several years and like everyone else had wondered if the man would ever give love another shot. The fear in his eyes spoke volumes, and Carl hoped the young woman being secured to a backboard would be alright.

"We'll use the helicopter because the quicker we get her into surgery, the better off she'll be. I've got the people I need here on the ship, but not the facilities. If we wait, we'll have to deal with traffic, and that makes me crazy."

Carl and Cam both nodded because CeCe was notorious for her boisterous frustration with traffic. It was one of the reasons they weren't seriously considering a move back into the heart of the city.

"Is she going to be okay?" Tucker's question hadn't been asked of anyone in particular, and he hadn't taken his eyes off Mia when he'd spoken. CeCe turned and grasped his hand to gain his attention.

"She's going to be fine, Tucker. I was able to clamp and repair the worst of the vascular damage. But it's a patch, and it needs to be fixed properly in a sterile environment. I know you soldiers are all about battlefield medical care, but I'm a little more particular about my patients. She needs surgery and a lot of TLC, which I'm going to leave to you and your brother. She's going to be fine, I promise."

Carl had watched CeCe deal with frightened families many times, patiently repeating the same assurances several times, yet she never seemed to become frustrated with the need to say the same thing again and again. He'd asked her about it once, and she'd explained she repeated what they needed to know until she saw the light of understanding in their eyes. He'd never fully understood that until tonight. Tucker hadn't heard her reassurance the first time, but the second time his shoulders had sagged with relief, and there'd been an unmistakable sheen of unshed tears and relief in his green eyes.

Fifteen minutes later, the helicopter lifted off. The pilot promised to return for Brock and Tucker if he could get clearance, and Carl hadn't been able to hold back his laughter at the incredulous look on Cam's face.

Yeah, I don't think clearance is going to be a big problem.

Chapter Twenty-One

TALLY STARED AT the letter in her hand as a wave of anger, unlike anything she'd ever experienced, moved over her. She'd never believed anyone actually saw red until this moment. The world around her was being filtered through a red haze that hadn't been there a few seconds ago.

If you had asked her a year ago how she would react to what she'd just read, she'd have been able to answer without a moment's hesitation. But now? Now the object of her anger wasn't here for her to rage at, and she had no idea if he would ever return.

Accepting his death had been difficult for so many reasons, but she'd finally come to a place of peace. Then the pictures arrived, destroying the fragile first steps she'd made to put her life back together again. There'd been so many emotions to sort through, she'd felt like she was drowning for the first several weeks. The only reason she'd made it through relatively unscathed was the man who'd held her together when grief and guilt had threatened to pull her under.

Knowing her husband had kept this secret was almost as painful as knowing how far they'd drifted apart.

"Why wasn't I enough?"

Koi's arms came around her, and he pulled her back into his chest. She hadn't even realized she was shaking until his strength stilled the shudders racking her body.

"Ma poupée, I don't want to ever hear you say that again, are we clear? You are more than enough. You're brilliant, loving, kind, thoughtful, funny, and beautiful. Your lively spirit draws people like moths to a flame. You think of others before yourself, and you give until there is nothing left if I don't watch you closely." He turned her and hugged her close, pressing her ear against the center of his chest.

"You hear that? That's the steady beat of a heart I thought would never find a woman to love before I met you. When Karl approached me about becoming your third, I knew there was more to it than that—it was written all over his face. I didn't hesitate because I was already fascinated with you, and we'd only seen each other in passing at Kodi's wedding. We hadn't even been introduced, and I was caught in your sweet web."

Koi's words were always a balm to her soul. Time after time, he'd held her when everything she thought she knew fell away to rubble. He'd shown her in a million little ways how much she meant to him, and so many times, Tally had worried she was the only one getting anything meaningful from the relationship.

"He always told me the time wasn't right... that he didn't want children until we were ready, and he was never ready. I gave up a lucrative career in Washington to move to Montana, and I never regretted that sacrifice because it so quickly became the home I'd never had. The majestic beauty was only part of its appeal. The people here are real, they say what they mean and mean what they say.

"I put off having a family because he'd sworn it would be worth the wait even though he knew how much it meant to me. At one time, he'd even talked about having a vasectomy, so he could play the sympathy card with the public. *Woe is me because my lovely, professional wife and I can't have children.* When in reality, he didn't want a child to interfere with his career. He was convinced children would hold him back politically, and God forbid if they weren't absolutely perfect in every way."

KOI COULD FEEL the emotion roiling through Tally, and as much as he wanted to calm her, what could he say? Her husband had fathered a child with another woman—a woman who had written to thank him for helping her shortly before he'd left on a trip that sent everyone associated with him into a tailspin. She needed to burn off the excess energy before she could deal rationally with her emotions. Letting her go off the rails now wouldn't serve anyone well.

"Here are your choices, love. Kickboxing, swimming, or we can spend the rest of the evening in the playroom." As much as he would enjoy losing himself in her for the next few hours that wasn't what she needed most.

Taking a deep breath, he was pleased when she only hesitated for a couple of seconds before answering. He'd spent months building her trust, assuring her he meant it when he gave her choices, that he wouldn't lay them out if he wasn't perfectly fine with whatever she chose. So often she'd worried everything was a trick question, and she was being set up to fail. For that alone, Koi would gladly kick Karl's ass. What had appeared on the outside to be an idyllic marriage had evidently been anything but.

"Kickboxing and I don't want you to baby me. After we've finished, I'd like to eat greasy tacos and snuggle." He smiled down at her and kissed her forehead.

"I have no intention of babying you in the ring, *ma poupée*, but I am going to make sure you burn off some of the anger I see in your eyes—it's cheaper than bail money." She laughed as he'd hoped she would as he led her up the basement stairs. When she reached the top, she turned so she could look directly into his eyes.

"Thank you." He must have looked surprised because she laughed softly and shook her head. "Obviously, I don't say it often enough if it surprises you when I express my gratitude." She drew in a deep breath, and he wanted to erase the sadness clouding her eyes forever. When he opened his mouth to respond, she placed a finger over his lips. "I love you. I fall a little deeper every single day. You empower me when I feel the most broken, and you always manage to bring out the very best in me."

Koi was stunned by everything Tally had just said. He'd been careful to not push her over the past year but had decided a few days ago he needed to find a way to tell her how he felt. Smiling to himself, he was grateful she'd been a step ahead of him. Brushing back a wayward strand of her pale blonde hair, Koi hoped he could find the words that would do justice to the depth of emotion he felt.

"I love you, too—more than I can tell you. I'm humbled you see me the way you do. The only other women who have ever loved me unconditionally are my mother and sister." And it was true, he'd never had a woman of his own. He'd topped a lot of submissives over the years, but there had never been one he wanted to keep.

"When I first moved back to Montana, I wasn't in a very good place. I was disillusioned with a career I'd always known could only end one of two ways. Either I'd get hurt and be forced into retirement, or I'd make a bad call and die in some dark alley in bum-fuck-nowhere. The government would never acknowledge I'd even been there, and Kodi would be left dealing with nothing but unanswered questions and endless red tape."

It was true. Aside from his sister, his life hadn't felt like it really belonged to him for so long, at times, he'd wondered if he would be able to find the man he'd once been. Warm fingers brushing over his cheek brought him back to the moment. Koi smiled at the love he saw reflected in her bright blue eyes. Karl Tyson had been a fool, he'd failed to recognize the treasure he'd had and thrown it all away. If the rumors floating through the intelligence community were credible—and they usually were—the man hadn't even been faithful while he was trying desperately to convince Tally to marry him.

"Let's go kick some ass. We'll both feel better, and we'll be able to enjoy those heavenly tacos without guilt."

He agreed with her, they both needed to expend some of their pent-up frustration. He needed to stop regretting what he'd lost and live in gratitude for all he'd been given, and she needed to come to grips with Karl's betrayal before deciding where she'd go from here.

Karl was currently recovering under a cloak of anonymity at a world-renowned drug rehabilitation clinic in Antigua, one of the few in the world on the leading edge of the new designer drugs and those being developed to allow the manipulation of cognition. Pharmaceuticals had long been used on prisoners of war, but technology had advanced to a point where it was dangerously easy to program another human to do your bidding. In Koi's opinion nothing good could come from these drugs—nothing!

Koi had stood aside and let the Wests subtly discourage

Tally's inquiries about visiting Karl in Antigua. He'd suspected she would eventually remember the letter, and he'd been right. Learning he was still alive had been the push her subconscious had needed. It had been damned hard to stand down and let everything play out, but he'd wanted her to be in charge of her own destiny. He'd support her decisions, but ultimately, she needed to make them without his interference. She'd thanked him for empowering her. This was a large part of his effort to be sure she knew how strong she was, but it was damned hard to sit on his hands and watch her swim against the ever-increasing current.

They'd changed into workout gear and driven to their favorite gym in less than a half hour, and Koi was relieved to find sparring partners available for both of them. He didn't mind training with Tally, and he'd been a damned tough trainer when she'd needed that outlet over the past year. But he usually refused to spar with her because he never wanted to cause her anything but the sweet pain that led to a mind-blowing orgasm.

Kick-boxing was one of Koi's favorite forms of exercise; it required not only muscular strength and cardio-fitness, but there was also a significant strategic element that kept his mind sharp. He'd never doubted his ability to read his opponent's body language had helped him be a better Dom, and that alone, made it worth the effort.

His sparring partner today was Lee Barber, one of Brandt Morgan's deputies, and a member of the Mountain Mastery Club. Lee was a quick and intuitive kickboxer, and if Koi wasn't careful, he was going to get his ass handed to him.

"What's up with you, man? You're not usually this distracted."

Koi wasn't a fool. He knew Lee had just very politely told him to yank his head out of his ass and pay attention to what he was doing. Refocusing on his opponent, Koi fought the urge to interrupt their session, so he could check on Tally. Lee deftly maneuvered them around the ring until Lee's back was to Tally, ensuring his words wouldn't travel across the space.

"Brandt briefed us on the situation with Senator Tyson." This was one of the things Koi liked about former soldiers, they generally cut to the chase fairly quickly. "How is Dr. Tyson coping?"

"It's been a challenge for her. She'd finally accepted his death, then she was hit with the news he might still be alive."

"I can see where there would be a lot of unwarranted guilt associated with not knowing he was alive while he was being held prisoner."

Koi didn't respond because he had the distinct feeling the other man wasn't finished. They continued circling the small ring, and Barber waited until he once again had his back to Tally before speaking.

"When I decided I wanted to resign my commission, Uncle Sam took it upon himself to reassign me for the last six months."

Koi had sparred with Barber a few times, but they hadn't talked much outside the ring, so this was news. "And?" Since Koi knew the other man wasn't simply reciting his resume, he was anxious to hear what he had to say.

"At the time, the Secret Service was actively recruiting, and when they didn't get any takers, they pulled in short-timers. I was assigned to the Senate for five months." The look in the other man's eyes told Koi this wasn't information Barber intended to share in public, but before he could say so, the man grinned. "Like I said, unwarranted guilt. Dr. Tyson stitched me up a few months ago after I had my skiing accident. Nice lady. She deserves better."

Koi made a mental note to talk to the Lee Barber privately, then nodded in agreement.

"She certainly does."

Chapter Twenty-Two

BROCK LEANED AGAINST the cartoon decorated wall of Mia's room and sighed. The décor might remind him of an elementary school, but there was no doubt the facility was a top-notch surgical center. Cam had proudly explained CeCe had built the hospital and attached clinic from the ground up, and Brock had to admit, it was damned impressive. Seeing Dr. Cecelia Barnes in doctor mode was something to behold. She was the perfect blend of professionalism and compassion, and it had been easy to see the staff here adored her.

Mia had been drifting in and out of awareness since returning from surgery. CeCe had assured them she would come around quickly because the surgery had gone perfectly, and they'd been able to complete it with minimal anesthesia. Brock hadn't known until after the helicopter lifted off the ship that Tucker had been injured as well.

Shifting his attention to the next bed, Brock shook his head at his brother's stubborn insistence Mia be the first one into surgery. The bullet that had passed through her shoulder had lodged in Tucker's upper arm. It still had enough velocity to embed itself in the bone, but miraculously, it had slowed enough the bone hadn't shattered, thank God.

Pushing away from the brightly decorated wall, Brock moved to Mia's side. Leaning down, he pressed a soft kiss to her forehead and whispered, "The two of you are going to be the death of me."

"The people we love can be a real pain in the ass." Brock turned to see Kyle West standing inside the door, a knowing grin curving his lips. "The right woman will drive you insane, and it goes without saying, younger brothers are the bane of our existence." Since they were twins, Kyle was mere minutes older than his younger brother, but from what Brock had heard, he never let Kent forget who'd been born first. The door opened beside Kyle, and Kent stuck his head into the room and grinned.

"Hey, I resent that remark."

"Doesn't mean it isn't true." Kyle's smile made Brock chuckle, and he appreciated the Wests' attempt to lighten his mood. Kyle looked at him and nodded toward the door.

"Take a break, I'll sit with them. Tobi is waiting outside to take you to dinner. Kent will drive, we don't need to fill up the rest of this floor with accident victims."

"I love her to death," Kent chuckled, "but her driving terrifies me. I swear she is almost as bad as Mom." Brock felt his brows raise in surprise because Lilly West's horrendous driving was the world's worst kept secret.

"Thanks, I'm hungry, and I know I need to get out of here for a while. Since they're both resting and out of danger, I'm going to take you up on your offer. CeCe said they can return to Prairie Winds in a couple of days if all goes well."

Ten minutes later he was riding the elevator and listening to Tobi list all the reasons she should be allowed to drive. Kent patiently countered every point, but the little blonde bundle of fire wasn't going down without a fight.

"I thought you said this was my car?"

"It is your car. Ownership is not the issue," Kent's even

tone didn't seem to appease his frustrated wife.

"I want to drive."

"Noted."

"So, you'll let me drive?"

"No, I just wanted you to know I'd noted your request." Kent looked over her head and grinned at Brock. Obviously, the man was going to push her to the tipping point.

"It's not fair, you know. Brock isn't afraid to ride with me, are you?"

He was grateful she didn't wait for him to respond because there was no way to answer the question without stepping on someone's toes.

"He's been in countries where cars get blown up every day. Riding with me will be a walk in the park. You weren't over in BFEistan mothering him, so why are you all cranky about it now?"

BFEistan? What the fuck? Shaking his head, it took Brock a couple of seconds to realize Tobi had combined Bumfuck Egypt and the last part of the various Middle Eastern countries where U.S. soldiers were deployed.

Brock enjoyed Kent and Tobi's company at dinner, smiling at their easy banter and watching in amazement as she charmed everyone they came into contact with. By the time they were on their way back to the hospital, she was giggling from the two glasses of wine she'd had and repeatedly promised to make sure their small cabin behind the club was fully stocked with the snacks she knew Tucker liked and a basket of toiletries for Mia.

Kent assured him they were also revamping the security around the small cabin he and Tucker shared. "We'll have additional perimeter alarms in place by the time you arrive. The new recruits are jazzed about the prospect of setting it up."

"And Lilly offered to ride shotgun if you need her for the trip home." Tobi grinned and winked over her shoulder at Brock when Kent let loose with a litany of curses worthy of his former career as a sailor.

"Tobi, you are forbidden from telling my mother anything about their travel plans, do you understand? The last thing we need is her anywhere in the vicinity as they make their way home. Hell, maybe we should fly you back to avoid Hurricane Lilly."

"She's not that bad, she's more of a tropical storm than a hurricane. You shouldn't exaggerate. I don't think she's ever shot anybody who didn't deserve it, and she's only blown up one boat."

Brock could see her chewing on her bottom lip as she thought back, and he was forced to muffle his laughter with a cough.

Tobi finally returned her gaze to Kent and added, "You know she didn't shoot that guy on the hill across the river. She shot the snake beside him, and the big coward jumped off the cliff into the water all on his own, so you can't count that one. And I heard Cam is the one who blew up the boat in the gulf. Your mom was totally jealous of that missile thing, she wants one for Christmas."

"Jesus," Kent's muttered curse was the final straw. Brock didn't know if it was the topic or the fact he'd finally relaxed for the first time in days, but it felt damned good to throw his head back and laugh until the muscles in his stomach ached.

CAMERON BARNES LEANED back in his seat and stared at the

agent sitting across the table from him. Why would the Agency send an agent—so wet behind the ears, he was practically dripping on the carpet—to deliver the bullshit explanation about Tyson's captivity? It was as baffling as it was insulting.

"So, you see, Mr. Barnes, there's no need for you to waste any more of your valuable time on this matter since the agent had gone rogue several months before Senator Tyson's plane went down. The agency clearly had not had any stake in the Senator's captivity, and everyone is relieved he managed to escape. Of course, we're looking forward to debriefing him as soon as possible." And there it was, the bait Cam had no intention of taking.

"Where is your rogue agent now?" Cam was tiring of this verbal sparring match; not only was it a waste of time, it was bordering on insulting. It was time to put a little pressure on this sacrificial lamb. The man's face paled, and he was suddenly fascinated with his fucking fifty-dollar shoes. *Christ, when did the Agency stop hiring operatives with at least minimal fashion sense?* His phone vibrated in his pocket, and Cam pulled it free to check the message.

He has ugly shoes. You should give him pointers. Cam was going to paddle her ass. Cecelia and Carl were sitting on the other side of the small bistro waiting for him to end this fiasco, so they could go look at a house.

The agent cleared his throat before answering. "We tracked him to Costa Maya where he rented a boat. After that, the trail goes cold." *No shit. I think you'll find it's damned difficult to track someone who's been blown to hell over water.*

"Well, that's unfortunate because it seems bringing him in would be an agency priority. If it was my op, I'd be very interested in how a rogue agent was allowed to supervise the captivity and drugging of a U.S. Senator for months without anyone in the Agency questioning his whereabouts or making an effort to find out what he was up to."

Cam wasn't sure what was going on, but the corruption in the organization he'd devoted most of his adult life to was growing exponentially. He planned to stay as distant as possible, but if they brought it to his door, Cam wouldn't stand idly by and watch them hurt anyone he cared about.

An hour later, Cam pulled the car to a stop in front of the large home Lilly West had told him was for sale. The owners wanted to keep the sale private, and he was relieved they wouldn't be dealing with a pushy realtor today. After his meeting with the Agency flunky, he wasn't in the mood.

Lilly stepped from the front door, and Cam smiled when Cecelia all but ran into the older woman's arms. Lilly West was one of those rare people both men and women adored; she was also a trouble magnet like none other. Kent had warned him Lilly had announced she wanted a handheld rocket launcher for Christmas, so Cam was prepared for her to badger him about their availability.

Cam had already worked out a compromise he hoped would satisfy her curiosity without endangering half the state of Texas. He'd arranged for her to spend the day at the Camp Bullis Training site north of San Antonio. Ironically, Lilly's reputation had already filtered far enough into military lore, the Commanding Officer was happy to arrange her visit. Now all Cam needed to worry about was convincing Kent, Kyle, and their fathers Lilly wouldn't be given free rein with the armaments.

Before they reached the top of the stairs, Carl pulled

Cam aside.

"Was that asshole the best the CIA had to send? Hell, even from across the room, I could see he was a fucking stooge." Cam didn't even try to hide his amusement. Carl might submit to him, but the man was as Alpha as they came in every other aspect of his life.

"Christ, I hope not, or we're in a hell of a mess."

Chapter Twenty-Three

Brock knew Mia was standing silently in the short hallway between the small cabin's master bedroom and kitchen, listening as he and Tucker discussed Joseph Moreno's recent disappearance. Her bare feet had been nearly but not completely silent on the wood plank floor. Smiling to himself, he was grateful she still hadn't figure out how difficult it was to sneak up on former SEALs.

They'd managed to keep her isolated in their cabin for the past several days, claiming she needed time to recover, but that was coming to an end today. Tobi and her entourage could only be held off for so long, so he and Tucker had finally agreed to a late afternoon picnic before the club opened. Whether or not they played at the club depended on how Mia and Tuck felt after dealing with a group who could be overwhelming on their best day.

Tucker cleared his throat and gave a quick nod toward the hall, letting Brock know he was also aware of Mia's presence. Without making a sound, Brock rose from where he was seated and padded silently to the back of the kitchen. Shaking his head, Tucker kept talking while Brock stepped into the back of the hall behind Mia.

"Cam assured me they'd be at the picnic tonight, evidently he has a gift for our sleeping sub."

Brock snaked one arm around Mia's torso from behind in a move so quick, he knew she hadn't had time to react.

He pressed his other hand flat over her chest to ensure she didn't make any movements that might tear open her incisions. The stitches were removed yesterday, but the tissues were still tender, and he'd seen his fellow soldiers rupture newly healed incisions when they'd done too much, too soon.

Her startled scream brought Tucker around the corner, and Brock smiled at his brother's worried expression. Whispering over the sensitive shell of her ear, Brock felt her body relax for a fraction of a second before stiffening for an entirely different reason.

"Eavesdropping isn't necessary, baby. We won't keep secrets from you when the information involves your safety. Your breakfast is in the warmer, but before you eat, let's chat about what you're wearing."

"Kodak, are you wearing something under this shirt? I thought we'd made our dislike of panties crystal clear." The corners of Tucker's lips twitched in amusement despite the sharp tone of his voice.

Brock almost laughed when she lifted her chin in defiance before answering.

"I have on panties. You can't expect me to eat without panties. It's undignified and unsanitary."

"Unsanitary? We've both had our tongues buried so deep in your pussy, we could feel your vaginal walls contracting as you came. We lapped up your sweet cream as it pulsed over the sensitive taste buds—and you think we're concerned about sanitation? No, sweet cheeks, we want to be able to play with you while we eat. And since you didn't bother to follow directions, you're going to eat without the shirt as well."

Brock felt her stiffen in his arms and laughed softly as he bent down to kiss the side of her neck. "Consequences, baby. Actions have consequences. Ordinarily, you'd be over one of our knees, but your body isn't recovered enough for that yet." Tucker wouldn't be able to hold her securely yet, and there wasn't a chance in hell he'd let Brock have all the fun.

Tucker led Mia into the kitchen, and Brock readjusted himself. Just being near her made his cock stand up and pay attention. Having her deliciously curved ass pressed against his crotch had not only drained most of the blood from his brain to his raging hard-on, it had also made him fantasize about marching her right back down the hall and not letting her out of bed until she agreed to stay with them. Since Mia's father had been a U.S. citizen, there were no immigration hurdles for her to overcome—something they'd been relieved to learn.

Brock smiled when he finally rounded the corner into the kitchen and found Mia sitting beautifully bare, sipping orange juice. Tucker had adjusted her legs, so her feet were hooked around the legs of her chair, opening her pretty pink pussy to their view. One of the first things he'd noticed when he moved to Prairie Winds was the Wests penchant for glass tables. It had seemed at odds with the western décor, but it hadn't taken him long to figure out why the two men preferred the more modern tables.

The first time Brock had eaten dinner at the main house, he'd struggled to keep up with the conversation surrounding him because his friends had provided plenty of distractions. He'd been sitting across from Gracie and watching Micah and Jax bring her to orgasm during dessert had almost made Brock come in his damned pants—something he hadn't done since he was a teenager. He'd have known what the men were doing to their sweet sub without the front row seat but adding the visual component had certainly made his first dinner memorable.

Tucker was seated on Mia's right, and Brock took the seat on her other side. He'd always preferred sitting across from his dates during meals, but it was going to be different with Mia. The closer they could keep her, the easier it would be to show her how perfect they'd be together. It had taken everything in him to keep from hiding her backpack when Cam returned it to her at the hospital. He'd never cared when a woman said she was leaving—hell, he'd usually been the one to walk away, but with Mia, everything was different.

"Are there any leads in Joseph Moreno's disappearance?" Mia whispered the question without taking her eyes off her plate, and after what they'd discovered on her laptop, Brock wasn't surprised.

"Were you going to turn him in, Kodak?" Tucker had been furious when he'd read her notes. She hadn't gathered enough information to go to the authorities prior to being whisked out of Colombia, but there had been enough to convince the team of the man's guilt.

"Yes, but things in Colombia aren't the same as they are here. There is so much corruption there." Brock wasn't entirely convinced she was right, but he wasn't going to argue the current political climate of either country. "My grandfather trusts him, I'd say he probably counts him as a friend. What Joseph is doing is wrong, and I have to find a way to tell my grandfather." Her eyes went glassy with tears, and she bit her lip to stop it from trembling.

Tucker pulled her onto his lap with his good arm and held her close as Brock brushed his hand in slow strokes from her wrist to her shoulder. Mia's tanned skin felt like warm silk beneath his hands. The scent of sweet hibiscus floated around him as her skin warmed. Hell, he was never going to be able to walk through a botanical garden again without getting a hard-on. He didn't vary the pace, keeping the movements smooth to help slow her breathing, which had accelerated so much, he'd wondered if she was going to hyperventilate.

"Sweetheart, Joseph Moreno isn't going to be a problem for you or your grandfather ever again." Brock was thrilled to finally be able to give her some good news. "General Moreno had an accident while caving." She tipped her head in confusion, the adorable action had him fighting a grin. One of the newbies on the team had gone caving in Mia's home country a few years ago. When Sam McCall had given the team the go-ahead to take out the man, the team hadn't wasted any time making sure his body would never be found.

Once they'd confirmed Mia's suspicions, no one felt any guilt about ending his human trafficking days. Moreno and his merry band of deviants wouldn't ever hurt another child. Granted, they'd only eliminated one cell in a huge network, but if it saved one child, it was worth it. It might not be a huge dent in the problem, but to the kids who had been returned to their families, it meant everything. When they'd finished explaining everything to her, Mia flashed them a smile that lit up the entire room.

"That's poetic justice because the man was terrified of caves. I overheard him talking to my grandfather one time about some of his men who were into it. He was convinced they'd never be seen again."

"Well," Tucker grinned and drawled, "sweet cheeks, seems that might have been more of a prophecy than you realized."

Brock felt some of the tension drain from his own muscles as he watched the interplay between his brother and the woman who'd started wiggling herself into his heart before they even met. Watching Mia from a distance in Colombia had been as frustrating as it had been fascinating. Damn, even the way she frowned at her laptop late into the night when she'd been editing photos had turned him on.

He could hardly wait to see her reaction to Cam's surprise this evening. Sending up a silent prayer she'd see it as a sign and agree to stay with them, he lifted her from Tucker's lap and nodded down the hall.

"Go get dressed, baby. We're going shopping." When she frowned, he gave her bare ass a solid swat. "That wasn't a request, sweetheart." She shot him a look that earned her a couple of swats later, but for now, they needed to get her a pretty dress for this evening.

Kent West had chuckled when he'd recommended the store in Austin.

"They have a great selection of edgy clothing that's just this side of club wear. Their sales staff is helpful, but they'll know when to leave you alone in the dressing room. Those changing rooms are large enough for three people, and they're soundproof, too."

For the first time in as long as he could remember, Brock was looking forward to shopping with a woman. And if anyone told his little terror of a sister, he'd have to shoot them because there was no way he was shopping with Nell.

"I SWEAR THEY are worse than shopping with my grandmother," Mia blinked back tears of frustration and slipped another damned dress over her head, "and she wrote the book on picky... God rest her soul." She wasn't speaking ill of the dead, she really wasn't. It was just a fact her sweet grandmother always seemed to think you needed to try on everything available in your size and a couple of others before making a choice. Mia was more of a pull it off the rack and hold it up in front of you shopper. If it looked like it might be just a bit baggy, it was perfect... or at least good enough.

She stepped out of the enormous dressing room and sighed when she came face to face with the most patient salesclerk in the world. The woman hadn't batted an eye as Brock and Tucker rejected dress after dress for petty reasons that had Mia ready to push them off the top floor of the department store.

One of the things she'd always enjoyed when traveling was seeing the tall buildings. Historically, Colombia had too many earthquakes and too few advancements in engineering for buildings to be over three or four stories. That had been changing for the past couple of decades according to her grandfather, but the sheer number of skyscrapers in foreign cities still fascinated her.

Pulling her thoughts back to the present, she smiled at her mind's meandering and once again, thought about shoving them off the roof if they rejected another dress. Stepping in front of the triple mirrors, Mia could see Brock and Tucker shoot to their feet. They'd been slouched in the chairs where they'd been waiting for most of the past hour, but the moment they saw her, they'd both risen and stalked toward her. Tucker's low whistle made her smile despite her earlier homicidal thoughts.

"Fuck me, Kodak. You look amazing."

"We'll take this one and the shoes, in addition to the other things we've already picked out."

Other things? What other things? Mia didn't understand what Brock was talking about, but one look told her he hadn't been talking to her. The sweet attendant smiled and nodded in understanding before turning away from them.

Brock's gaze locked with hers in the mirror and the sinister smile that spread over his face might have alarmed her if she hadn't been able to read the heat in his eyes.

"Baby, this dress only needs one thing to improve it."

Blinking her eyes several times as she tried to make sense of his words, she finally broke free from his intense stare to look down at the pretty cornflower blue sundress and wondered what he could possibly think was missing because it already seemed awfully skimpy to her.

"Let's go." Brock wrapped his enormous hand around her upper arm and moved through the door of the dressing room. Before she could turn around to look for Tucker, she heard the door of the dressing room close and the lock engage.

Brock and Tucker stood in similar poses, feet spread shoulder width apart, arms crossed over their massive chests, their eyes blazing with heat.

"Take off the dress, baby."

"I thought you liked it?" She could hear the trembling in her own voice, but she wasn't able to calm her nervous reaction. She'd been worrying all day they were simply being polite and making certain she had clothes for the return trip home.

"I do like it. That's why I want you to remove it because if I do, it's going to be in tatters around those pretty fuck-me sandals. Now, take it off." When her eyes filled with tears he frowned.

Her hands were shaking so violently, no matter how hard she tried, Mia couldn't get her trembling fingers to grasp the zipper pull at the side of the form-fitting dress.

"You still want me?"

TUCKER'S FINGERS HAD closed over Mia's, stilling hers because he was worried she was going to tear the fabric. Gently pushing her fingers aside, he'd almost finished unzipping her dress when he heard her question. Tucker was shocked, and it was clear by Brock's expression, he was equally stunned. Tucker grasped the wrist closest to him and pressed her palm over his straining erection.

"Oh, sweet cheeks, I defiantly still want you."

The glare Brock gave him made Tucker chuckle. Christ Almighty, did his brother really think he was that dim? *I probably don't want to know the answer to that question.* Lifting the warm hand caressing his engorged cock to his lips, he pressed a lingering kiss to her palm.

"Don't ever think our interest in you was tied to the mission."

Brock grasped her other hand and pulled her close.

"You are intelligent, talented, sweet, and loyal. I can assure you, our interest in you hasn't diminished because it appears you're safe."

"Not only are we grateful you are safe," Tucker chuckled, "we're also damned relieved we can focus on convincing you to stay rather than spending all our time worrying about every fucking creak and moan the cabin makes all damned night. I'm looking forward to sleeping a little more soundly now that I'm not worried about the boogeyman sneaking in and carrying you off into the night."

Mia giggled at his ridiculous comments as he'd hoped

she would, but she quickly sobered, and Tucker leaned forward to where she stood in the circle of Brock's arms. Caressing the side of her face, he sucked in a breath as a tidal wave of emotion swept over him. Mia's dark eyes and sweet floral scent were a siren's call he couldn't resist. Her dark eyes were filled with such a wide range of emotions, he could almost feel the way they swirled inside her. He saw confidence warring with fear as trust battled doubt, but it was the hope and love that drew him like a moth to a flame.

Last night when the three of them had been cuddling on their soft sofa while watching old movies and munching on popcorn, Tucker had found a sense of peace he'd never dreamed possible. When they'd offered to take Mia out on the town, she'd politely asked if they'd mind spending the evening at home.

Tucker had been such a fool marrying a woman he'd known was more interested in partying than building a family together. His pride had overridden his usual level head, and he'd mistaken lust for love. And he'd been an even bigger fool for trying to build a wall around his heart to cover up his mistake.

Looking into Mia's gorgeous blue eyes, Tucker saw the future he thought he'd lost and thanked the Universe for giving him another chance and showing him what he'd been missing.

"You're a gift I don't deserve, sweet cheeks."

He watched as her eyes filled with tears she valiantly held back as she shook her head.

"I don't want to hear you say you are unworthy because it's not true. My grandmother always reminded me I shouldn't measure my worth by another's scale, and I don't think I truly understood what she meant until now. You can't blame yourself for another person's mistakes, and you shouldn't feel unworthy because she failed to appreciate what an amazing person you are."

Tucker pressed a kiss to her plump lips and smiled. "Thank you, sweet cheeks. You are a treasure—an overdressed treasure."

He and Brock stepped back in a well-coordinated moved that might well have appeared choreographed to anyone watching.

"Strip, baby. We're going to play a bit before we wrap this shopping trip up and head home."

The slight tremor of Mia's fingers as she slipped the thin straps of the sundress from her shoulders was the only indication Mia was nervous about the order Brock had given her. Tucker held out his hand and she didn't hesitate to place the garment in his outstretched hand.

"You are temptation personified, sweetheart," Tucker agreed, and now that he'd admitted how much she meant to him, he had no intention of letting her go.

Chapter Twenty-Four

MIA WAS DROWNING in sensation, and she still couldn't still her mind. Brock's hands were cupping her breasts, lifting them as if testing their weight, then rolling her nipples between his fingers, pinching the tight peaks, and sending flaming arrows of need to her pussy. She unconsciously arched into his touch, pressing her shoulders against Tucker's chest. The feel of his soft cotton shirt brushing over her bare skin was amplified, knowing she was completely exposed and they were both still fully dressed. *Not fair*.

"What's not fair, Kodak?" Tucker's warm breath wafted over the sensitive shell of her ear, and she moaned as her desire ratcheted up several notches.

Brock's sharp pinch to her nipples made her gasp and reminded her she hadn't answered his question.

"You're both still dressed and..." her voice faded when Brock lowered his mouth to the torrid peak and lashed her nipple with the tip of his tongue. The heat made her cry out as she teetered on the precipice of a cataclysmic release.

"Who is in charge, sweet cheeks?" Tucker's question was followed by the scrape of his teeth over the tender slope between her shoulder and neck.

"You are. You and Brock, but—"

"No. There is no *but*—your only responsibility during a

scene is to submit. You don't need to worry about anything but following our commands. Your pleasure belongs to us—it feeds ours." Tucker's voice was raspy, and Mia had come to recognize the change as an indication of his arousal. It was gratifying to know he was as affected as she was.

Brock went to one knee in front of her, and Mia moaned in anticipation. Since meeting the Deitz brothers, she'd learned a lot about the lifestyle, but she wasn't naïve enough to believe she was anything more than a beginner.

"Spread those pretty legs for him, sweet cheeks." Tucker's words might have bordered on seductive, but she recognized them as a command. Her legs parted before he'd gotten the words out, and she was rewarded with dual growls of approval.

The tip of Brock's tongue slid through her drenched folds, Mia's knees started to tremble, and she worried they would fold out from under her as heat seared over every inch of her skin. She felt her womb contract in response to his oral assault, sending a rush of her cream to greet him.

"Fuck, baby, you taste like a sweet, juicy, exotic fruit. All this smooth skin slick with your own lube is testing my control, but I think it's time to change things up a bit."

BROCK HELPED HIS brother position Mia over the leather padded bench positioned discreetly at the side of the dressing room and made a mental note to thank Kent West for recommending this store. He was confident they would be doing a lot of business here in the future. Unzipping his pants and freeing his throbbing cock from its confines, he breathed a sigh of relief until he felt Mia's warm breath brush over the sensitive flesh of the head.

"Jesus, Joseph, and sweet Mother Mary." Brock hadn't realized he was standing close enough he'd be able to feel her warm sigh, and the sensual feeling pulled the rest of his available blood south, making him sway closer.

"Look at this beautiful ass. Smooth skin over rounded globes that fit my hands perfectly and between them lies paradise."

Brock appreciated Tucker's attempt to distract Mia because it had been a monumental mistake on his part standing close enough for her to be able to trace her tongue along part of his corona. She was stealing his control, and the little minx hadn't even taken him into her mouth yet.

"Suck me, baby, while your other Master slides so deep, you won't know where he ends and you begin."

Her moan vibrated all the way up his spine before sending spears of heat out in every direction—hell, his toes curled inside his boots, the pleasure was so intense.

"Get her there, brother, because I'm not going to last long. Her mouth is pure magic." Mia's body lurched forward as Tucker pushed deep, and Brock felt her gasp around him.

The wet sounds of Tucker pulling from her soaking pussy combined with the hot sounds of Mia humming around his cock edged Brock closer and closer to release. Reciting every math table he'd ever learned in school wasn't doing anything to distract him from the mind-numbing pleasure swamping his senses. Watching Tucker reach under her to pinch her clit was a profound relief. Brock wanted them to all come at the same time, and he'd been much too close for things to last much longer.

Mia's mouth clamped down on him and went from hot

to flaming in a split second. He watched her entire body tense, and from the tortured look on Tucker's face, Brock assumed her pussy had contracted like a vice around him, too.

"Come for us, baby." He'd barely uttered the words when she shattered. Brock had to brace his hand against the wall to keep from falling, the pleasure so intense as he shot hot pulses of his seed to the back of her throat. Mia swallowed around him, and the added pressure made him shout out her name.

Brilliant colors burst behind his eyelids, and for the first time he could remember, Brock was afraid he might not be able to stay on his feet. He'd never been with a woman who affected him the way Mia did. Every time they played, the pleasure was more intense than the time before. *At this rate, she's going to kill me sometime Sunday.*

Thirty brain-fogged minutes later, the three of them and a backseat full of packages were loaded in Tucker's truck on the road back to Prairie Winds. Mia glanced over her shoulder and sighed.

"You spent too much money. When I get access to my accounts, I'll pay you back, but grandfather has probably locked everything up. He'd see it as a security issue if he knows I've left the country."

Neither Brock nor Tucker were going to say anything about her grandfather because that issue would be resolved sooner rather than later, but he wasn't about to have her think she was going to pay them back.

"Paying us back isn't going to happen, sweetheart. Money is never going to be an issue between us."

"But you are soldiers, right? Does your military pay that well?" He could hear the sympathy in her tone and wanted to laugh.

"Sweet cheeks," Tucker snorted and shook his head, "we are former SEALs and you are right, no honest soldier ever gets rich defending his country. We're a part of the Prairie Winds team now, and even though they pay a lot better than Uncle Sam, we're doing it because it's what we love, not because we need the money."

Mia's confused expression was so adorable, Brock was tempted to leave the situation well enough alone, but she deserved an explanation.

"Baby, you aren't the only one with a grandfather who made a lot of money in finance. Our mother's family traces their history in banking back six generations."

"And each of those generations considered it their family duty to set up trust funds for those who followed. Money isn't an issue for us, either," Tucker's words were true, even if they were an understatement. Neither he nor his brother had ever touched their trust funds, but for the first time, Brock was considering it, he'd love to purchase a home for the three of them to share.

KOI LED TALLY out to the end of the dock at Prairie Winds and turned her, so they stood face to face. They were on their way to visit Karl but had accepted the Wests invitation to stop over for a couple of days before flying on to Antigua. They planned to attend the picnic starting in a few minutes, but he'd wanted this to be a private moment between the two of them. Brushing back a strand of pale blonde hair from the side of her face, Koi wished he could erase the shadows he saw in her eyes.

The Tally he'd finally coaxed out from under a blanket of grief and guilt had been absent since the pictures arrived several weeks ago, and he prayed the next few days brought her the resolution she deserved.

"*Ma poupée*, I wanted a moment alone with you before we fall into Tobi's crazy, chaotic world. There are some moments that deserve the peace that can only be found away from others and near the soothing energy of flowing water."

Tally grinned at him and nodded. She'd installed numerous water features in her home during the past year, and they'd had several discussions about the power of water to cleanse the air around troubled souls. She'd lamented the fact they couldn't do the same in hospitals, and they'd laughed at how mortified Ryan Morgan would be by the suggestion.

"The peace it brings is unlike anything else in the world, and this is a lovely place. Thank you for sharing it with me. I love Tobi, but it's nice to have a moment before I'm confronted with all her energy."

Tally's sweet laughter bounced off the water, and Koi was grateful he'd decided against sharing this moment with their friends. His sister had surprised him by approving the quiet moment rather than a more public one she could have shared. Kodi had been a gift from God from the moment their parents brought her home from the hospital. Before meeting Tally, Kodi had been the only woman other than his mother who loved him unconditionally, and a piece of his heart would always belong to her.

"I want to ask you a question before we leave tomorrow. It's important that you know whatever happens in Antigua, nothing will change how I feel about you. Nothing will change the depth of my love for you. I want to spend the rest of my life standing beside you. I want to wake up beside you every morning and fall asleep with you wrapped in my arms every night." Tears were already racing down her pale cheeks, and Koi brushed them aside with his thumbs as he framed her face with his hands.

"I want to be your refuge, *ma poupée*, the place you're always safe when the world is closing in on you. I'll slay the dragons breathing fire at your heels when you're too spent to outrun them." He was deliberately leaving out references to their lifestyle because contrary to what he would have told you a year ago, he now understood that was only a small part of what he wanted in life.

For years, Koi had believed being a Dominant was who he was, erroneously seeing himself through blinders because it was all he felt he was capable of giving a woman. Contrary to what Tally believed, she'd given him far more than he'd given her; she'd taught him what it was like to love from the depths of his soul, and there wasn't a greater gift on this side of heaven.

In the distance, Koi could barely hear the nearly silent whir of a camera and was thrilled Mia Mendez had agreed to capture their special moment. In many ways, it was fitting and brought them almost full circle since it had been her pictures that changed the course of Tally's life and made this moment possible. Their trip to Antigua would give Tally a chance to ask questions he knew were always simmering below the surface, and as difficult as it was going to be, she deserved the opportunity to close that part of her life with a clear conscious.

Koi pulled a small velvet box from the inside pocket of his jacket and got down on one knee.

"I want to grow old with you. I want to sit on our porch watching our grandchildren play in the yard and smile when I remember all the twists and turns our lives took to get us there. I want our story to be an inspiration to our children and grandchildren, so they always know the power of star-crossed miracles. Will you marry me, Tally?"

"Yes. A thousand times yes." She pulled him to his feet and wrapped her arms around him in the sweetest hug he'd ever received. In a flash of insight, Koi saw his future and knew he'd get another hug much like this one before walking their daughter down the aisle. Stepping back enough to slip the diamond ring he'd commissioned for her on her finger filled his heart with more joy than he'd believed he was capable of feeling.

He was content to simply hold her and absorb the soothing sounds of the river moving past them on its way to the Gulf. In many ways, it was fitting because life was an ever changing, ever moving force he'd spent too much time fighting. It was time to slow down and float with the current for a change.

As they made their way back to the gazebo where Tobi stood waiting, he couldn't contain his smile when the little bundle of energy his friends called their wife began squealing and bouncing up and down. Kent shrugged his shoulders and chuckled as Kyle rolled his eyes.

"We kept her contained, but it wasn't easy. You're on your own now."

Koi had spent so many years isolated by the career choices he'd made, it felt good to be able to share this moment with friends. Looking around as Tobi gushed over Tally's ring, Koi sent up a prayer of thanks to his ancestors for their guiding hands and the gifts the Universe had given him. He might not believe he'd earned them—but he certainly wasn't going to turn them down.

Chapter Twenty-Five

MIA COULDN'T HEAR Koi's words, but that didn't keep her from understanding the depth of his devotion and love for Tally, it was written in every nuance of his body language. The hope and sincerity in his eyes were so stark, Mia had to blink back her own tears to continue capturing their special moment. She'd broken down and sobbed when he'd asked her to take pictures as he proposed. Knowing she'd get a chance to present Tally with another set of pictures felt like a second chance. This time, the photos would reflect a new beginning rather than tearing apart the other woman's hard-fought efforts to rebuild her life.

She knew she'd gotten some amazing pictures, but the one of them walking hand in hand toward the brightly lit gazebo was already her favorite. Seeing them silhouetted against the lights was symbolic of the bright future that lay ahead of them, and for just a moment, she was filled with an overwhelming sense of longing. She might not know what the future held for her, but Mia vowed if fate handed her the chance to stay with Brock and Tucker, she wasn't going to let it slip through her fingers.

Joining the party, Mia was happy to sit to the side, watching as Koi and Tally accepted the congratulations and best wishes of their friends. She'd never experienced the level of friendship playing out in front of her and part of her longed for those deep and enduring connections. Her family's wealth had been isolating, but necessary in a country being torn apart by warring cartels. She felt a pang of sadness; watching the country she called home slowly change into something barely recognizable was heartbreaking. Warm fingers caressing the side of her face broke through her moment of melancholy.

"What put that sad, wistful look in your eyes, baby?" The concern in Brock's chocolate brown eyes pulled her fully back to the moment, and she smiled though she doubted he was fooled.

"I'm sorry, I got lost for a minute. I don't want to bring any sadness to Tally's joyful moment." He nodded, but she knew the topic would be revisited. She'd never met men more adamant about knowing what was going through a woman's head that the Doms she'd met. When she was finally able to look away, she met Cameron Barnes' intense gaze. Did the man ever simply look at someone? Or did he always peer into the depths of the other person's soul?

Cameron's knowing assessment wasn't intrusive, but there was no mistaking it for anything other than what it was either. When she unconsciously leaned against Tucker's shoulder and grasped Brock's hand under the table, a smile ghosted over Cam's lips, and he gave her an almost imperceptible nod of approval. The moment was broken when a commotion on the path leading to the gazebo drew everyone's attention.

Turning to see what everyone around her was smiling about, Mia grinned when she saw Lilly West striding down the path, a bright smile lighting up her beautiful face as her husbands steadied her on the uneven surface. She navigated the cobblestones in three-inch heels as if it was little more than a minor inconvenience.

Mia met Lilly several days earlier and had immediately fallen in love with the vivacious woman who apparently adopted everyone remotely attached to Prairie Winds. As she watched the Wests approach the gazebo, her attention turned briefly to the couple following them, and she gasped in surprise. Mia stood so quickly, her chair teetered precariously before Tucker reached behind her to keep it from toppling over.

"Grandpapa?" Her feet were moving before the question had finished echoing in her mind. As she approached, Mia was stunned by the change in the only member of her family who hadn't been taken from her too soon. The man facing her looked completely different from the one she'd known in Colombia.

Gone was the gruff exterior and the harsh look of a man whose life was mired in a cutthroat business he was continually trying to navigate with as much integrity as possible. As an adult, Mia had finally been able to see how difficult his life had become. In place of the hardened shell of a man stood one exuding warmth, his arms spread wide, waiting for her. Running into his warm embrace, she was overwhelmed with his open display of emotion. Mia could count on one hand the number of times he'd shown her even the smallest gesture of affection in public, but this time, he'd been ready and waiting for her.

"My sweet, Mia, I'm so happy to see you. Knowing you'd escaped safely was the biggest relief of my entire life." When she pulled back, unshed tears glistened in dark eyes so much like her own, and it seemed the pain of the past and emotional distance between them melted away in the time it took him to whisper, "I love you so. I'd have never forgiven myself if Joseph hurt you." Her grandfather sighed, his eyes moving to her side, and she was surprised to see Cameron Barnes standing next to her.

"As usual, Cam's timing is impeccable. I've never known exactly how he does it. I tried to tell your grandmother he was a demon, but she always swore his halo was untarnished." The laughter that surrounded them brought a glare from Cam which was completely lacking in any semblance of commitment. The two men embraced, and Mia was struck by the realization they knew each other far better than she'd been led to believe. *Casual relationship my ass.*

The woman who'd been walking hand in hand with her grandfather smiled at Mia, a light-pink blush staining cheeks creased with the lines of laughter and a life well lived. She looked nervously at Lilly who gave the other woman a reassuring pat on the arm just as Lucia Mendez turned his attention back to her.

"Ellie, I'd like to introduce you to my single greatest accomplishment, my granddaughter, Mia. Mia, this is Eleanor Wishcoff. Ellie and I were quite an item once upon a time." Now it was Mia's turn to blush. Geez, there were some things she just didn't want to think about where her grandfather was concerned. He must have read her thoughts because he laughed out loud, and Mia stared at him in wide-eyed wonder.

"I haven't heard you laugh since before grandmother died." Her heart squeezed, and she was grateful for the warm arm that came around her shoulders. *Tucker.* She couldn't begin to express how sweet the sound of her grandpapa's laughter was or how grateful she was to the woman who'd obviously enchanted him. Pulling the surprised woman into a crushing hug, all Mia could manage to get out was a halting, "Thank you."

When she finally released the poor woman, Mia was

laughing and crying at the same time, overcome with relief, gratitude, and love. While Cam and Lilly introduced the pair to everyone, Mia found herself surrounded by Tobi and the other ladies she'd met at Prairie Winds. Tobi hugged her fiercely and smiled.

"Damn, sister. You don't do things half-assed, do ya?"

Mia's confusion must have shown because the other women rolled their eyes and laughed. CeCe stepped forward and explained.

"Let me interpret for our little Texas hellion. She means you're facing a lot of changes in a really short period of time. The part she hadn't gotten to before laying the slang on you was that we're ready and willing to help in any way we can."

Jen McCall leaned in and whispered, "Of course, our help usually involves margaritas and various levels of shenanigans, depending on who made the drinks and how well supervised we are. But we've got your back even if there's no booze. Probably."

Mia couldn't hold back her laughter and it felt remarkably liberating.

TUCKER WATCHED AS one emotion after another raced over Mia's pretty face. She was being steamrolled, and there wasn't a damned thing he could do about it. *Yet*. When Lucia Mendez asked to speak with her alone, he and Brock had both shaken their heads. She belonged to them and neither he nor his brother planned to stand back and let her face her grandfather alone. It was clear Lucia Mendez wasn't the same man she'd known, and after their conversation with Cam earlier today, they knew she wasn't in any physical danger, but that didn't mean the elderly man couldn't hurt her soft heart.

Brock sat on her right, taking her small hand in his as Tucker settled on her left, placing his hand gently against the small of her back. Lucia let his gaze flicker between them for several second, studying them closely before smiling.

"My darling Mia, I'm happy to see your young men appear to be as devoted as Cam assured me they would be."

"Grandpapa, I don't think you asked to speak with me to discuss my... rela... frie..."

Tucker shook his head when it became clear Mia didn't have enough confidence in their relationship to call it that. He felt her tremble against his side and decided he wasn't going to wait until later to dispel her doubt.

"Mr. Mendez, my brother and I are committed to protecting Mia, but we also want her to remain in the United States with us. Our relationship is just beginning, but rest assured our interest in her goes far beyond just being her bodyguards. Even though we seem to be facing a challenge convincing her, I'm confident we'll get there, eventually." *Hopefully, before she gets on a damned plane.*

"I'm leaving Colombia, Mia."

She stared at her grandfather in utter disbelief. Tucker's public declaration had surprised her, but her grandpapa's words made her head spin.

"As I was being wheeled from my home into the waiting ambulance, I wondered if I was dying, and I realized it wasn't going to be much different from the way I'd been living since I lost your grandmother. I loved the challenge of building a business that made me more money than I'd ever dreamed possible, but what good is money if you don't share it? Money isn't meant to lay in vaults for decades when it could benefit so many others."

Mia had been begging him for years to set up a foundation that would serve the medical and educational needs of the people of their home country. She argued education was the best way to keep the young boys from being lured into the cartels, and healthy children held the key to the future of their beautiful home. His chuckle drew her attention, and she felt her cheeks flush.

"I see you are remembering our heated discussions, but I want you to know, I was listening. Even when you didn't believe your words were getting through this thick head of mine, they always echoed with truth."

When his eyes flickered to where Ellie stood nearby, Mia's heart melted when she saw the love that had been missing for far too long. He took a deep breath and returned his attention to her.

"Mia, I'm selling the banks, the estate, and most of the other properties I've acquired. It was wrong of me to try to force you into a life you were never suited for. I want you to know the joy of doing what fills your heart and soul with joy. I want you to fall asleep at night knowing you've given everything in you to further your dream. But most of all, I want you to know what it's like to love and be loved. Your heart is too big to be kept hidden behind brick walls and iron gates. Denying the world the opportunity to see itself through your eyes would be a travesty. The future belongs to those who can see themselves as others see them and adjust their sails to steer in the right direction."

Mia's head was spinning so quickly, she was grateful

for Brock and Tucker's grounding touch. How had a few pictures changed so many lives so much? *If the picture of Senator Tyson could set all this in motion, how much more could I do in the future?*

A deep male chuckle beside them pulled her from her musing. "You have to love a woman who speaks their thoughts aloud." Kyle West's expression was equal parts amusement and indulgence.

"It's one of God's gifts to men, otherwise we wouldn't have a chance in hell of knowing what was going through their complicated minds." Kent stepped up beside his brother, giving her a quick wink that made her giggle and brought growls from both Brock and Tucker.

"I'm pleased you're asking yourself those questions Mia because my brother and I would like to discuss how your skills could be used by the Prairie Winds teams."

She felt Brock and Tucker stiffen beside her, making Kent and Kyle both laugh.

"Don't worry, sweetness," Kent grinned at her, "we'll deal with your men."

"And we'll help. My friends and I are formidable allies, and we'll help you all we can." Tobi stepped around her husbands, giving Mia the moment of breathing room she needed. Tobi introduced herself to Mia's grandfather, and looping her arm in his, walked him away to introduce him to the others gathered around.

Staring blankly at her grandfather's retreating back, Mia felt the brush of a warm breeze caress her cheek and smiled. Her grandmother had always reminded her the brief kiss of the wind was a kiss from heaven. The warmth that filled her heart settled her, and she felt her soul re-center itself as all the possibilities spread out in front of her started to shine like new coins.

"I made myself a promise on the ship that I wanted to experience everything I could. At the time, I thought it was just about the pleasure and learning about the Dominant/submissive lifestyle I'd read so much about. But now? Now, I want to amend that promise and add as many experiences and adventures as I can. I want to know I'll never feel as though I sat on the sidelines and watched as my life played out around me." She took a deep breath and sighed before continuing. "But most of all, I want to make a difference. I want others' lives to be a little better because I tried."

Chapter Twenty-Six

KARL STARED OUT the enormous window, watching the woman he called his wife for most of a decade walk down the cobblestone path and out of his life. The past year and a half had changed him in ways he'd never anticipated, and it had been easy to see how much Tally had changed as well. For the first time since he'd met her, Karl had been honest with Tally—laying everything out on the table. He'd hated hurting her, but she'd have been hurt even more if he'd continued the charade. She deserved so much more than he'd given her... more than he'd ever been able to give her.

The man with his arm wrapped securely around her shoulder, holding her close as they made their way to the waiting car was the one she needed and deserved. Despite his best efforts to convince her, he'd always known she would never be happy in Washington, just as he would never be content living full-time in Montana. The only time she'd cried during the entire time they'd talked was when she'd slid the letter across the coffee table. The pain in her eyes had felt like someone shoving a spear through his heart. But in the end, he couldn't say he regretted what had given him a child he adored.

The letter Tally had found was from the surrogate he and his lover had contracted to carry their child. Aleta had written to thank him for paying off her student loans and arranging several job interviews with prominent investment brokers on the east coast. She'd started her MBA while pregnant, but devastating morning sickness had forced her to put her studies on hold until after baby Karlton made his debut. Now that she'd finished her degree and landed a great job, her whole life lay in front of her. The irony of her gracious letter being the small thread that unraveled the façade that had been his marriage wasn't lost on him.

Karl heard the door close behind him and knew without looking his lover had come to check on him. Tony's arms slipped under his own, and Karl felt the man who held his heart in the palm of his hand lay his cheek against his back.

"How did it go? I've been worried about you." Karl's eyes filled with tears as the weight of everything began pressing in. The staff at the rehab unit had assured him it would take time for his roller coaster emotions to return to normal; the erratic swing was the one lingering side effect of the drugs he'd been given.

It had taken several weeks for his memory to return, and just as the doctors had predicted, once it started, it came flooding back in a deluge. Standing at this same window, he'd watched a sleek black limo wind its way up the long drive. When the uniformed chauffeur opened the rear door and Tony stepped out, everything had come rushing back and the onslaught had been staggering.

Karl's knees had almost folded from beneath him as he watched the man who'd captured his heart walk along the smooth cobblestones toward the entrance. The sheer volume of information that burst into his mind was overwhelming, but it was his memories of the guilt he felt about Tally that had shaken him to his core.

One of the most difficult memories to accept was his decision to give Tally one more chance to change her mind about moving to Washington. He'd been convinced it wouldn't work, but he'd still been caught up in everyone else's plans for his future to care about what he was doing to the one woman who'd always given so much more than he deserved. Hell, even his own family had given up trying on him.

The argument he and Tally had was so ugly, he still felt the shame and humiliation of the hurtful things he'd said. Every accusation had been a reflection of his own guilt. In the end, nothing had been resolved, and the scene before he left for Colombia had left them both too angry for any hope of a reasonable discussion. He'd decided to put off confessing everything until he returned—and everyone knew how that had worked out for him.

"I'm better since you're here." His answer was the truth, everything was better when Tony was close. Karl had lived in denial for so long, accepting himself had been the biggest mountain he'd ever had to climb. His love for Tony wouldn't have derailed his political career, but the uncertainty surrounding the drugs he'd been given certainly would. The doctors at the clinic had warned him the life he'd had before would be impossible to recover, but he hadn't believed them until the moment his memory returned.

The drugs he'd been given would always cast a shadow of doubt over his ability to make well-thought-out decision, a weakness his political opponents could and would easily exploit. The cartel had planted a lot of troubling seeds in his thoughts, and Karl would be forever grateful Mia Mendez sent the pictures to Tally and not to the U.S. Government. The fallout from who knew what/when was a growing scandal that was slowly moving up the chain of command and Karl suspected it wouldn't stop until it reached some of the upper levels of the CIA and Congress.

Without a clear career direction, Karl had decided to write a book about his experience, and he'd already been approached with multiple offers for the movie rights. Tally didn't know it yet, but he'd signed over everything he owned in Montana over to her—it was the very least he could do after everything he'd put her through. Karl hadn't hesitated to sign the dissolution of marriage papers as well as negotiating to ensure she wasn't forced to return the insurance money Uncle Sam had paid out, knowing he was still alive.

Koi Green knew what Karl had done with both the house and the small ranch north of town he'd inherited several years ago. The other man had reluctantly agreed to keep the secret until after this meeting. Karl had wanted her to be able to confront him without her emotions being muted by a false sense of gratitude. He loved Tally, but he wasn't in love with her. The truth was, he'd never been in love with her, but he'd selfishly married her anyway because she'd been the perfect wife for an up-and-coming politician.

As time passed, it had become impossible for him to continue denying who he was. He'd made so many mistakes, all of them adversely affecting the one person who'd handed her soul to him on a silver platter. Seeing the depth of pain he'd caused Tally had been more painful than all the torture he'd endured in Colombia.

The web of lies he'd woven had already begun unraveling before his ill-fated trip. It had only been a matter of time before his house of cards tumbled down around him, and in many ways, he'd felt as if he deserved what he'd received at the hands of the opportunistic bastards who'd found him on that mountaintop.

Turning to face Tony, Karl smiled at the man whose world had been destroyed by his disappearance and then shaken to the depths of his soul when he'd answered the door late one night to find Jen McCall standing on his doorstep. Jen's former career working in the State Department made her uniquely qualified to deal with even the most sensitive subjects diplomatically, but there hadn't been any way to break even the most welcome news gently.

Karl had always liked Jen, and he'd been grateful to learn she'd been the one to speak with his lover. She'd teased him during a FaceTime call later that he was pushing the boundaries of their friendship, but he'd learned later she and Tony had become fast friends, much to her two dominant husbands' amusement.

"Is everything ready?" Karl was anxious to start his new life. Today's meeting with Tally had been the last loose end he'd needed to tie up before returning to the home he and Tony shared outside Washington. Much to his dismay, Karl was already fielding offers from several groups interested in hiring him as a lobbyist. He'd finished the preliminary outline for his book, and he was looking forward to a couple of weeks spent playing with his son. He'd missed too many of Karlton's milestones and had sworn he wouldn't miss another.

"Yes. The jet is waiting, and our sweet boy was napping when I left. You'll like his nanny, she's a gentle spirit, and Karlton adores her." Tony was the very definition of a gentle spirit, so Karl was amused by his description. Karl was looking forward to meeting the woman who'd rocked his son, kissed away his tears, and who Tony considered one of their most valuable assets.

"Will she ever forgive you?" Tony knew him so well; the other man knew Karl's ability to forgive himself was largely dependent on being reassured Tally would be okay.

"Yes. I'm not entirely sure I deserve it, but I'm damned well going to take it." Koi was perfect for her, and he'd meant it when he'd wished them every happiness.

He'd gotten through their entire meeting without shedding a tear until she'd hugged him at the end and whispered, "There will always be a special place in my heart for you. If you ever need a friend... call." Her sweet words had destroyed his control, and it had taken him several moments to regain even a fragile hold on his composure.

Shaking off the emotion, he smiled at Tony, "Let's go. I'm checked out and packed." He nodded to the small backpack sitting by the door. It felt strange to acknowledge he'd arrived weeks ago with nothing but the clothing he'd been wearing, and he was leaving with not much more. Tally insisted on sending him the personal effects she'd saved. He'd been humbled to learn she'd only recently sorted through and disposed of the papers he'd once considered important to save.

Karl had already said his goodbyes to the staff and doctors who'd cared for him, so once he stepped from the family meeting room, he walked briskly until he was stepped out into the sunshine. Taking a deep breath, he turned to Tony and smiled.

"I'm ready, babe. It's time to begin again."

Epilogue

Six Months Later

MIA GRASPED A small rock protruding from the face of the cliff and cast a quick, worried glance at the river twenty feet below her.

"Don't look down. Do that again and you'll sit this one out, Kodak."

It wasn't the first time Sam McCall had warned her to keep her eyes on her goal, but it was the first time he'd added the caveat of pulling her from the mission.

Son of a biscuit, she wanted to slap Tucker silly for teaching their teammates that nickname. The first time he'd called her that in a team meeting, she'd known she was doomed. The mischief had danced in their eyes, and she'd groaned some vague threat of revenge she'd paid for later that night.

"Stop worrying about the water and spider monkey your way to the top. This isn't any different from the training wall in the gym."

Mia was grateful for Sam's encouragement, he'd been the most patient trainer she'd worked with. He'd stepped in the first time he'd seen her reduced to tears when Tucker shouted at her on the obstacle course. Mia would never forget what he'd said to her that afternoon.

"You won't care when I yell at you to get your butt in

gear because it won't be personal. Sage and I learned some hard lessons training Jen, I'm not going to stand by and watch you go through that."

Reaching up for the next handhold, Mia shifted the heavy pack on her back, careful to keep the precious contents from crashing against the rock wall. The cameras she'd be taking would send the pictures via satellite back to Prairie Winds. Thinking about the teenager being held in a cave sent a surge of determination through her. She'd been working her fanny off getting ready for an assignment and today was her first test she knew was geared to a specific mission, and she wasn't about to let her fear hold her back.

"I thought you said she could swim?" Sage McCall's taunting question made her blood boil.

"Don't talk about me like I'm not dangling from the side of a rock pile right below you. I swear to Pete, I'm going to take a blow gun and shoot you with poison darts when we go to BFEistan."

"I'm going to paddle Tobi's ass for teaching her that." Dammit, she'd forgotten about the com unit she was wearing. Casting a quick glance down to where Kent West watched from a nearby boat, she breathed a sigh of relief at the boyish grin on his face. God in heaven she loved the Prairie Winds team. "Make it worth her time, Mia. Show us what you can do."

Kent's words of encouragement were all it took, Mia scrambled to the top in record time. Crouching down after reaching the top, she surveyed her surroundings, anticipating the unexpected, just as she'd been taught, but nothing could have prepared her for the sight that greeted her.

Standing a few feet away, Brock and Tucker leaned against a truck loaded with luggage and bags of equipment. Kyle West stood closer to her with his arms crossed over his chest. His pose was formidable, but his smile put her at ease.

"Well done, Mia," Shifting his gaze to Sage, Kyle nodded, "you might want to check her gear for those poison darts. You're wheels up in an hour." Mia almost felt bad when the men all cringed at her happy squeal. *Fruit salad, I really need to remember these blasted com devices.*

LAKYN DROPPED TO her knees, huddling in on herself at the side of the road, trying to protect her bare arms and legs from the blowing dirt and small rocks pelting her. *They said it was windy, but no one said anything about this. Holy fucking hell, this is nuts. At this rate, there won't be any need to worry about being recognized because I'm not going to have any skin left.* She'd heard about the wild Texas wind, but she'd never imagined anything like the hurricane threatening to sandblast the top several layers from her body. *Should have stayed in the car. Should have stayed in the car. Shit. Shit. Shit. Why didn't I stay in the fucking car?*

She hadn't wanted to stop because, invariably, she was recognized at hotels, either by the staff or another guest, and within minutes, the place was crawling with photographers and fans. It defied logic if you asked her, she barely recognized herself without all the crap the studio's makeup artists plastered on her face. When she looked in the mirror, she saw Lakyn Hicks; the rest of the world saw Lakyn Storm.

Her manager was going to have a stroke when he figured out she'd slipped out from under his watchful eye. *Right, more like Scrooge guarding his investment.* She didn't care, she'd needed a break, and the woman she'd been talking to online had graciously offered her a place to stay if she was ever in Texas. Of course, she only knew Lakyn as the younger sister of one of her husband's former teammates. *I hope she doesn't think I misled her... but I guess I did. Damn, is this fucking wind ever going to stop?*

Lakyn loved her brother to distraction, but she wasn't naïve, Cooper was a player of the first order. Any woman getting involved with Cooper Hicks was doomed to heartache. Her brother was going to be pissed when he found out she'd driven across country alone. For some reason, he was convinced she was the same girl who got lost in the woods behind their family home when she was four.

It had been ten-year-old Cooper who'd found her battered and bruised at the bottom of a small ravine. He'd carried her up the steep incline and over a mile before other searchers spotted them and pulled her from his exhausted arms. In Cooper's mind, Lakyn would always be the helpless little girl he'd carried to safety.

Shaking her head, she blinked as beads of sweat rolled into her eyes. Hiding beneath her heavy jacket had seemed like a great idea when all she'd been worried about was the vicious sting of blowing dirt. Now, she wondered if it was possible to suffocate under lined nylon. Suddenly, using the coat as a shelter didn't seem like the stroke of genius it had a few minutes ago. *Should have stayed in the damned car.*

JUAN RIVERA TURNED to his longtime friend, Trac Hughes as he slowed to get a better look at the Mercedes parked at the edge of the road.

"What the hell? Who leaves their fancy ass car along

the road in this wind? There won't be a speck of paint left on the passenger's side by morning."

"I didn't see anybody in the car, so they probably called for their auto club. Hell, nobody would try to walk in this. You know this is blowing up a fucking storm. Keep going, I want to get to the club before it hits."

Juan continued driving but something about the abandoned car continued to plague his thinking. A couple of miles down the road, the hair on the back of his neck was standing on end as he fought to see through the blowing dust crossing the highway in reddish-brown clouds. He barely caught a glimpse of what looked like someone dropping to the ground before his view was obscured again. Slowing, he edged closer to the side of the blacktop while being careful not to run over whatever was huddled a few yards ahead.

"What the hell is that?" Trac was leaning forward, but it was Juan who jumped from the truck as soon as it rocked to a stop. As he approached, he could hear a muffled voice, but whoever was hiding beneath what looked like a winter coat didn't respond when he asked if they needed help. *Who the hell wears a winter coat in Texas?*

The question was quickly erased from his mind when he moved to block the wind, lifted the coat, and looked into the most beautiful eyes he'd ever seen. The unique variations of blue reminded him of the deep violet lilacs his mother loved so dearly, but the deep outer rings faded to the palest blue he'd ever seen. The effect was haunting, and his breath caught when the woman blinked in surprise that quickly morphed to fear when he didn't speak for several seconds. Before Juan managed to speak, Trac's booming voice sounded over the howling wind.

"What the fuck, Rivera? If it's a critter, you're not picking it up. No more fucking strays, our place is already a damned zoo." As a former Special Agent with the FBI, he and Trac had worked together for longer than Juan wanted to think about.

The angel with the beautiful eyes pulled the coat back over her, ducking out of sight.

"Damn it, Hughes, you scared her."

"Her?"

"Yeah, her as in person. Two legs, not four." Pulling the coat back up, Juan smiled and held out his hand.

"Come, *Chiquita*. Let's get you out of this wind before we all get run over." Standing on the edge of the highway wasn't safe, and he was anxious to get back in the truck because once the lightning started, the danger would increase exponentially. Juan was relieved when she finally laid her small hand in his. Her fingers were so small and delicate in his palm. The bolt of electricity that streaked through him made him suck in a quick breath.

Helping her to her feet, Juan had the strangest feeling he'd seen her somewhere, but her face was so smudged with dirt, it was difficult to tell. She was petite, the top of her head barely reaching his shoulder, and she was wearing a ridiculous pair of heels. When she stumbled against him, murmuring an apology, he heard Trac swear, "Holy shit."

Before Juan could ask Trac what was wrong, the woman surprised him by asking, "Do you know Tobi West?" When he and Trac both stopped and stared at her, the woman ducked her head and grimaced. "Sorry, I was hoping perhaps you knew how close I was to her house. She told me if I was ever in Texas, I was welcome, and well, I was hoping to surprise her. She said her place was… well, special. You know… safe." *Safe?* Why did the angel with the beautiful eyes need a safe place?

Without answering her question, Juan took her hand in his and led her to the truck. Opening the driver's door, he lifted her effortlessly into the center of the seat.

"Yes, *Cariña*, we know Tobi. We were headed to Prairie Winds ourselves." He wanted to smile at the pink blush that spread beneath the dirt smudges on her cheeks. Obviously, she wasn't completely clueless about Prairie Winds.

"What's your name, darlin'?" Trac's southern accent was more pronounced when he was aroused, and Juan was relieved to see he wasn't the only one attracted to her.

"Lakyn. Lakyn Hicks." She'd added her last name so quickly, Juan couldn't help glancing over her head at Trac and raising a brow in question. The shit-eating grin on his friend's face should have been a clue, but he had no idea what Trac was chuckling about.

"Want to amend that, Princess?" This time Trac's voice sounded amused despite his stern reprimand.

"Damn," the whispered curse came just as Juan turned onto the long drive leading to Prairie Winds.

Pulling to a stop in the recently built parking garage, Juan turned off the ignition and turned in his seat to look at the pair sitting next to him. The smudged angel looked frustrated or guilty, he couldn't decide which while Trac looked like the cat who swallowed the fucking canary.

Juan had been mildly annoyed a heartbeat earlier because he hated feeling like an outsider looking in, but the defeated look spreading over her face brought his protective nature surging to the surface.

"Spit it out, *Cariña*."

Rather than answering him, she looked at Trac.

"Do you think she'll be angry?"

Now it was Trac's turn to look confused.

"You mean Tobi doesn't know who you are?" She shook her head, and Trac leaned his head back and laughed out loud. "Oh, this keeps getting better and better." Juan was losing patience with the side conversation, and his snarl of frustration drew his friend's attention. Nodding in his direction, Trac grinned.

"Juan Rivera, meet Lakyn Storm."

Lakyn Storm? Fucking seriously?

The End

Books by Avery Gale

The ShadowDance Club
Katarina's Return – Book One
Jenna's Submission – Book Two
Rissa's Recovery – Book Three
Trace & Tori – Book Four
Reborn as Bree – Book Five
Red Clouds Dancing – Book Six
Perfect Picture – Book Seven

Club Isola
Capturing Callie – Book One
Healing Holly – Book Two
Claiming Abby – Book Three

Masters of the Prairie Winds Club
Out of the Storm
Saving Grace
Jen's Journey
Bound Treasure
Punishing for Pleasure
Accidental Trifecta
Missionary Position
Another Second Chance
Star-Crossed Miracles

The Wolf Pack Series
Mated – Book One
Fated Magic – Book Two
Tempted by Darkness – Book Three

The Knights of the Boardroom
Book One
Book Two
Book Three

The Morgan Brothers of Montana
Coral Hearts – Book One
Dancing with Deception – Book Two
Caged Songbird – Book Three
Game On – Book Four
Well Bred – Book Five

Mountain Mastery
Well Written
Savannah's Sentinel
Sheltering Reagan

The Christmas Painting

I would love to hear from you!

Website:
www.averygalebooks.com/index.html

Facebook:
facebook.com/avery.gale.3

Twitter:
@avery_gale

Made in the USA
San Bernardino, CA
30 April 2018